SWEAT

Stories and a Novella

Lucy Jane Bledsoe

Seal Press

Cover and text design by Clare Conrad
Cover photograph by Debra LaCoppola

Acknowledgments: "Solo" was originally published in *Another Wilderness*, edited by Susan Fox Rogers, Seal Press, 1994. "Sex Is an Ancient Practice" was originally published under the title "Sex! Ancient Practice Revealed" in *Girljock*, May 1992.
The following stories were previously published in slightly different forms: "State of Grace" in *Women on Women 2*, edited by Joan Nestle and Naomi Holoch, Plume, 1993; "The Pass" in *Evergreen Chronicles*, June 1993 and *Sportsdykes*, edited by Susan Fox Rogers, St. Martin's, 1994; "The Night Danny Was Raped" in *Sister and Brother*, edited by Joan Nestle and John Preston, HarperSanFrancisco, 1994; "The Rescue" in *Beyond Definition*, edited by Marci Blackman and Trebor Healey, Manic D Press, 1994; "Teamwork" in *Dykescapes*, edited by Tina Portillo, Alyson, 1991 and *Growing Up Gay*, edited by Bennett Singer, The New Press of New York, 1993; "The Place Before Language" in *Afterglow*, edited by Karen Barber, Alyson, 1993.

Library of Congress Cataloging-in-Publication Data
Bledsoe, Lucy Jane.
Sweat: stories and a novella / Lucy Jane Bledsoe.
ISBN 1-878067-64-8
I. Title.
PS3552.L418A6 1995 813'.54—dc20 95-16106

First printing, September 1995

Distributed to the trade by Publishers Group West
Foreign Distribution:
In Canada: Publishers Group West Canada, Toronto, Ontario
In the U.K. and Europe: Airlift Book Company, London

ACKNOWLEDGMENTS

Many people have supported me through this book adventure and I am grateful for their contributions and love. First and foremost, thanks to Patricia Mullan for more than I can possibly name here. Thanks to Shannon Smith for her dream about my book, to Katie Deamer for sharing the adventures of the trail, to Susan Fox Rogers for hours of priceless consultation, and to Nisa Donnelly for telling me about kidney beans and much more.

A huge thank you to the members of Bad Books—Katy Ross, Herb Wiseman and Patricia Mullan—with whom I have shared books, great food, and exceptional parties for twelve years. And to the readers who have given me crucial feedback on these stories, including Jane Adams, Linnea Due, Paula Ross, Canyon Sam, Debra Slone, and Deborah Stone. I am also grateful to the Barbara Deming Money for Women Fund for providing timely support.

Working with "the Seals" has been a joyful experience. Many, many thanks for the warmth and inspired work of my editor Holly Morris and her cohorts at Seal Press.

For Patricia for absolutely everything

CONTENTS

STATE OF GRACE

WHEN I WAS FIFTEEN I believed that sex was nearly the same thing as softball. The feelings were the same anyway. I fell seriously in love for the first time during a double play. Charlene played shortstop and I played third base. We led by one run and it was the bottom of the ninth, bases loaded, one out. We had to win this game to go on to the State Championships, so when the best hitter in the league, probably in all of New Mexico, stepped up to home plate I got scared. On the first pitch she belted a one-bouncer right between Charlene and me. Charlene called for the play and snagged the ball while she dove through the air horizontal to the ground. Even before her body thudded into the dust she scooped the ball to me at third. I tagged up and fired it to first base for a flawless double play. We'd won the game. I looked at Charlene and fell instantly in love, deep in love, and could tell by the fervor in her eyes that she had too. In the exact same moment.

The next thing I did, after falling in love, was look for Michael in the stands. He was my best friend and primary coach. He also happened to have been living with my mom for the past seven years. Scanning the bleachers I found him sitting alone, far from Mom, and remembered that they had broken up last week. A fireball of anger and sadness tore through my stomach, but I discharged it by thinking of Charlene and the double play. It was as if Charlene rolled like a boulder right into the spot where Michael had been. All in about five seconds.

After the game the rest of the team went straight to Galluchio's for pizza. Charlene and I lingered in the locker room, said we'd be right along, but didn't hurry. First I couldn't pull myself out from under the shower nozzle where the water slid down my body in dozens of hot rivulets. Then I wanted to take my time with the lotion, getting each toe and between my shoulder blades. Finally dressed, Charlene and I walked slowly back to the softball diamond, just talking, not planning to go there but that's where we wound up. We walked deep into left field where the grass became patchy under the pine needles of the piñon forest. Twice Charlene had slugged homers into these woods. I liked to think about those two softballs that no one bothered to chase down, and wondered where they were now. Coyotes might have carried them off or they could be sinking into the forest floor, slowly decomposing, the earth sucking them in.

Charlene dropped down next to the first tree in left field, placed her hands behind her and threw back her head. I knew just how she felt. A hot dusk swelled up around us, and as I took deep breaths the smell of fresh cut grass raked through my chest. I laid my hand on Charlene's thigh to feel her shortstop muscles. Charlene picked up my hand and examined my callouses, touching them with the tips of her fingers. She said, "Here is the hand that can stop any hard-driven ball in the league. And you're only a sophomore." She lifted my hand to her mouth and ran her tongue along each callous, then licked the center of my palm, swirling her tongue in slow circles.

I waited a long time, as long as it took the full moon to rise over the top of the backstop, expecting Charlene, being a senior, to kiss me. When she didn't I kissed her.

Charlene was a loud, sturdy girl. She was tall, big-boned and had long dark hair which she usually wore in a ponytail or long braid. Her mouth and eyebrows seemed to jump off her face they were so aggressive, bold. She was team captain that year, gregarious and so brassy that some people couldn't quite take her. I could take all of her.

The funny thing about Charlene, though, was that when she wasn't cracking jokes and taking charge, she had a raw shyness. Hardly anyone knew that about her, but once you looked closely it was obvious. Her brown eyes, for example, even as she shouted some obscene remark across the shower room, always had a tentative glint. As long as we all kept laughing, Charlene kept performing, but she was ready, at any given moment, to back off. I was just the opposite. I was quiet most of the time, and people usually thought I was shy. Actually, I'm not shy at all. I have a way of going for what I want. That night, out in left field, when I pulled Charlene's face to mine and kissed her, she folded right into me. The moon climbed higher and higher as we lay on the borders of the softball field and the piñon forest, its light sanctifying every touch. Still, even then, it was all softball to me.

From then on, every day after practice we walked home together. She wasn't allowed over to my house, on account of the lack of supervision there, so we usually went to hers. Charlene's mother didn't like me. My mother let me do whatever I wanted, and I guess it showed. I wasn't wild or anything, just free. My hair looked like straw, bleached and dry and nearly the same color. I didn't comb it enough. My nose was usually sunburned and peeling. Besides the way I looked, I made Charlene laugh too much and we rarely did any homework. Also, when we walked home together we were often late because we liked to take the long woods route. The way we went there wasn't even a trail, just dry pine trees and thick, sweet air. One of us always found a reason to start wrestling even though Charlene established early on that she could whoop me. I liked lying on my back, afterwards, watching the clouds in the sky. I imagined they were giant beds on which Charlene and I floated. I didn't want to talk much at these times because I wanted to savor her salty softball taste in my mouth. Neither of us could wait until the middle of June when school let out.

The last thing I wanted to think about that spring was Mom and Michael's breakup. At home it was always in my face. In the mornings Mom didn't just leave toast crumbs all over the kitchen counter, she didn't even bother to brush them off her shirt anymore. She gained ten pounds, which was a lot of extra on Mom who was already big, and let her hair grow lank and long. She even cancelled a class she was teaching at the junior college. Suddenly we weren't even saying hello and goodbye, just coming and going in the house like two stray cats. Michael had moved out, or was thrown out, and was sleeping in the back room of his auto parts shop.

I didn't need to tell Mom anything about me and Charlene for her to get the picture. She had to know by the music I played, by my face every evening when I came home, by the fact that I *lost* ten pounds. Besides, I had an attitude a mile high. I believed I had surpassed Mom in the realm of Knowing About Love. Mom had left Michael because she'd discovered he was having his second affair (actually, it was his third but she didn't know this) in their seven years together. I pitied Mom for allowing herself to be abused like that. I knew that Charlene would never be unfaithful to me. I *knew* that. I knew it like I knew how to belt a ball into left field with the full force of my body. For the first time Mom's and my lives seemed to be forking off in different directions. I felt sorry to be leaving her behind.

On a clear Saturday morning in early June Charlene's mother opened the door to Charlene's bedroom and found me on top of her daughter, buck naked the both of us. I had been deep in softball at the moment, the smell of blue sky lying against the back of my throat, the dampness of spring soil between my legs, the strength of the best shortstop in the league beneath me. When I heard the door bust open I flipped off of Charlene and looked her mother dead in the eye. In that moment I learned that this wasn't softball at all. This was sex. I felt not fear but an overwhelming sadness that I would never again be able to confuse the two. Sex was fucking and I was doing it with another girl.

In softball there is one perfect moment. You are standing at home plate, the bat cocked over your shoulder, waiting for a pitch. You watch the pitcher's feet, the scuffle of dust, the strength in her calves as she winds up then lets fly. As the pitch comes your way you feel a surge through your groin, a racing of blood down your arms and into your wrists. You lead with your left arm, pulling the bat even and hard until that one perfect moment, exact contact with the ball, the *crack* of a well-hit pitch.

Ever since I was eight and Michael began teaching me baseball, that crack of the bat against a ball has been my mantra, a sound I hear when I want something very badly but can't express what it is. When Charlene's mom opened the door that Saturday morning and found me lying on top of her daughter, buck naked the both of us, my mind filled with the sound of bat-driven balls, one after another in quick succession, as if I were at some marathon batting practice. Perfectly hit balls flew from my mind and slammed across the dusty floor into the astonished gut of Mrs. Duffy.

Charlene's parents pulled her out of school that Monday. I heard the news from our coach, Mr. Kaufman. He looked miserable. "Charlene won't be with us anymore. She's taking her finals early and going on a trip with her parents. She won't play in the State Championships. Of course, we'll still go to the tournament. And," he added, not at all convincingly, "we'll still win."

I couldn't quite believe what I'd just heard.

When I called Charlene that night, her mother answered. "You are not to call here anymore, Kathy." She hung up. I called back.

"You'd better listen to me carefully." This time it was Charlene's father. He worked as a missionary on the Navaho Reservation. The family used to live on the reservation until their home had been vandalized too many times and they moved to town. Mom thought trying to be a Christian missionary among Native Americans was as sick as making nuclear bombs or raping women, but she tried to keep her opinions to herself when Charlene became my best friend. Of course I agreed with Mom. But I knew Charlene was different. Not many people got to see the authentic Charlene, she was buried so deeply under that loud voice and coarse language. The authentic Charlene knew remarkable things, but she carried her genius in her muscles. I could see it all when she played ball. I liked to think that one day Charlene would let the authentic Charlene take over. With a father like hers, though, I understood why she kept herself a secret. He said to me on the phone, "One more call to our household and there will be serious repercussions. We've decided, for Charlene's sake, not to talk to your mother or the school officials, but that will become necessary if you don't understand that—"

"You can talk to whomever you fucking want to talk to," I interrupted. I knew the difference between whom and who because Mom was a writer. "Put Charlene on the phone."

He hung up on me.

I wished he *would* call Mom. I needed her. Until this spring we had always talked about everything. She treated me like another adult, not only because I was all she had until we met Michael, but also because she believed children should be treated as full people. Mom does just about everything by principle. Or at least she tries incredibly hard to. She'll do anything to avoid making a mistake. I always figured that was because of the couple of big ones she made early on. First she hooked up with my father and then she had me. She hates it when I remind her that I was a mistake, because she says I'm the best thing in her life. I believe that, because she says so, but that doesn't mean I wasn't a mistake. "There can be good mistakes," I used to tell her.

Mom was in the next room and must have heard me shouting on the phone, but if she did, she ignored me, which never would have happened before Michael moved out. I kicked the wall a couple of times and still got no response from her. It struck me just then that Michael was gone, Charlene was gone, and now even Mom was gone. I felt too alone to even cry.

I met Michael when I was eight. He was driving a truck for Van Lines at the time and dating Sandra, another waitress at the truck stop where Mom worked. Sandra looked like those chrome decals on the mud flaps of trucks, big head of hair, size three waist, and huge pointy tits. She had about as many brains as those chrome babes have too. Though Michael was dating Sandra, he always sat in Mom's station at the cafe because he liked talking to her. The first thing I ever heard Mom say about Michael was, "He's so typical. Likes to talk to women with brains but have sex with airheads."

When Michael learned that Mom had childcare problems with me on Saturdays, he started taking me to ball games. Mom wouldn't have ever given Michael the time of day if I hadn't adored him so much, but we started going out for barbecue on Saturday nights after Mom's shifts and Michael's and my ball games, and before long they were sleeping together. I had never seen Mom so happy. It was as if Michael had reached in and turned her inside out. He was pretty ecstatic too. He'd never been with a serious woman and Roberta—my mom—is definitely a serious woman. He said it was the first time, since he was sixteen, that he'd been really in love.

Then Mom found out he'd never quit sleeping with Sandra. She canceled out her relationship with Michael like a check she hadn't meant to write. She could be that methodical and thorough. After that Mom managed to take a couple of Saturdays off and tried taking me to ball games, but they were no fun without Michael. Mom had no idea how to keep statistics and I hadn't yet learned enough from Michael to do it on my own. "We'll look for a class, Kathy," she had said. As if there were a class on baseball statistics out here in the New Mexican desert.

That was just the beginning. We ran into Michael in the grocery store a month after they broke up and I blurted out that I'd like to go to the ball game. At that age I didn't understand faithlessness and I pretty much blamed my deprivation of Michael and baseball on Mom. He instantly agreed to take me to a ball game and Mom fired him a vicious look. I thought she was being a bad sport.

I began to realize the extent of my power over my mother's life when, after Michael and I had gone to several ball games, she began seeing him again too.

Mom's first novel got published the following year. She began a second one right away. When that got published, her publisher sent her off on a reading tour. That's when Michael had his next affair, the one that Mom never knew about, though everyone else in town did. I was eleven. Michael was living with us by then. He'd quit driving the big rig and had opened his own auto parts shop. The whole time Mom was out of town he moped, at least around me. I think he wanted me to know how hurt he was that she'd left him for so many weeks. As if that would justify his affair. I was torn. I didn't think it was justified, but I loved Michael. I pretended I didn't know.

This third time (second to Mom's knowledge), there was no pretending. When Mom found out in the early spring she remained calm. She announced that Michael's problem was maintaining intimate relationships.

"Seems like he maintains too many of them if you ask me," I commented.

"Kathy, when a person is afraid of his own depth of feeling, he'll try to spread out his feelings so that he doesn't have to feel so deeply."

Mom repeated her diagnosis every day for a week, then she abandoned reason altogether and blew up. At first I was relieved. All that psychology talk made me nervous. Then I was frightened. Her rage hurled her into some kind of twilight zone that I thought she would never come out of.

When Charlene's parents censored Charlene from my life I joined Mom, attaching myself like a caboose to her rage at Michael. From what I could tell it was all his fault. If he hadn't cheated on Mom I'd still have a family. It was his bad luck that he chose the Monday following the Saturday in June that Charlene's mother discovered us in bed to come beg forgiveness of Mom. I heard it all because it took place in Mom's bedroom which is next to mine. Michael was so quiet through Mom's reasoned speech (she could pull off a show of rationality even at the heights of her fury) that I wondered if she'd killed him first. She finished in a low steady voice. Michael had to know that that voice meant now and forever dead to Roberta. She said, "I've loved you more than anyone in the world and I've given you every break I can think of. Now I don't want to ever see you again. This is a small town, Michael, so I'm going to ask you to do one last thing for me: respect my feelings. Please don't try to see me or call me. It's over and this time it's so final you could be a lead weight dropped in the sea's abyss as far as I'm concerned."

Leave it to Mom to be dramatic and literary even while ending the love relationship of her life.

I snuck out of my bedroom to watch Michael leave. His face was gray and slack. I'd never seen him cry, but I could tell he was going to now. "Michael," I said as he opened the front door. Michael is over six feet tall and he nearly cracked his head on the top of the door I'd startled him so. A tiny burst of hope skidded across his face. How many times had I saved him from Mom's fury? Well he had the wrong idea this time. I told him, "You deserve it, every single word. You're a slime bucket and the whole fucking town knows it." Then I just stared at him until he got up the courage to continue out the door and leave. I watched out the window and saw him drop his head down on the steering wheel. His back started heaving. I have to admit a very big part of me wanted to run out there and throw my arms around him. I loved Michael, but he had hurt Mom so badly I didn't know if I'd ever see her throw her hands on her hips and die laughing again. Even a smile seemed damn near impossible at this juncture. And me, I had no one. Not Michael, not Mom, and now not even Charlene. So I let Michael cry. I wanted him to feel the full extent of the damage he'd done.

The next day I stopped by his auto parts shop on my way home from school. When I walked in he looked so pleased to see me that I almost couldn't do what I'd come for. "Kathy! Here, sit down, want some coffee?"

Even then I knew my hatred was for Charlene's parents, not Michael, but that didn't stop me. I snarled, "Since when do I drink coffee?"

"Well, it's all I have."

I said, "Michael, you are not invited to any more of my games, including the State Championships. I want nothing more to do with you." I waited to see the agony register on his face.

"Sugar." He'd always called me sugar. "This is between your mother and me. It doesn't have to have anything to do with you and me. We've always had a separate relationship." Since being with my mother, Michael had learned all kinds of relationship-talk.

"It has everything to do with me," I said. "Roberta's my mother. You've cheated on her three times. You think I never knew about that second time, but I did. Everyone in town knew except Mom. If you can't control where you stick your dick then forget it. I don't want to see you at *any*, and I repeat, *any* of my games. Got it?"

Michael looked devastated. I was his only link to Mom and I knew he counted on somehow working his way back to her through me. He always had. Sometimes I thought Michael and I had been closer than he and Mom. We were definitely more alike. He claimed he got involved with Mom, back when I was eight years old, because of me. He said, "Any woman who could raise a daughter like Kathy, I wanted to know." Besides being his link to Roberta, Michael had taught me everything I knew about softball. He'd bought my first glove, showed me how to tie a softball in it and oil it for shape, and taught me how to keep statistics at games. He'd coached me for hours and hours and hours over the past years. I knew that my going to the State Championships was one of the proudest moments of his life. I intended to deprive him of it. For hurting Roberta. For hurting me. And because I missed Charlene so much that even my toes ached.

"What can I do?" he asked. "For god's sake, Kathy, what can I do?"

"There's nothing you can do. You've fucked up royally."

If I had known everything about love in April and May, I began to know a lot about loss by late June. A week before the State Championships I broke down. I called Michael at the shop. When he answered, "Main Automotive. Can I help you?" I just said, "Okay, you can come."

"Kathy!"

"Yeah."

"Hold on a minute." He must have put his hand over the receiver because I could only hear his muffled voice say, "I've got to take this call. I'll be with you in a minute." Then he was back. "To the games next weekend, you mean?"

"Yeah."

"Well, uh, great." Like, what else could he say? Then he thought of something. "Does Roberta know?"

"Know what?"

"That you said I could come."

"I didn't mention it."

"Oh."

"She doesn't own the ball park."

I could hear him smile. It was like I was dangling a bit of bait. My power to grease his way back to Roberta, if I chose to. "Right," he said. "You know I'll be there."

"Right," I answered, still all business. I wouldn't cut him much slack. I needed to have the feeling he was wrapped around my little finger.

"Kathy," Mom said the morning of the State Championship finals. We'd already breezed through the quarter- and semi-finals. "You're in some kind of trouble. I've been a bad mother. I'm sorry, but I'm just cracking up right now."

"Then crack." Why was she laying all this on me now? On the morning of the most important game of my life?

"You're in trouble, aren't you?"

"No more trouble than you're in." For the last two nights Mom had sat with Michael in the bleachers watching the quarter- and semi-finals. Both nights she came home, went to bed and cried. I'd never seen her so broken, nor so stripped of pride. Mom has pride even in private, even alone in her bedroom. I got the feeling she suddenly wanted to talk about my trouble now because hers had become so acute.

"What happened to Charlene? Why isn't she in the games?"

"Fine time for you to be asking," I answered.

"I'm sorry I haven't been here for you."

What could I say? In a way, Mom and I were going through the same thing. Only Michael had been a shit to her. Charlene had no control over what had happened to us. I felt superior to Mom, for having sense in whom I chose to fall in love with. So I sighed and said, "You got your own problems, Mom. Deal with them. I have a game to play tonight."

Mom looked bad, sallow and puffy. I sort of hated myself for not caring, for needing Michael for my own reasons.

"Well," she said. "It's only right of course that Michael should come to the games." She said this as if it were a conclusion to the discussion we'd just had about her and me.

"It's the principle of the thing," I said, sarcastically tossing her one of her own favorite expressions.

Everyone turned out that night for the State Championship finals, which by luck were held in our town. The Lions sold hot dogs, popcorn and sodas. The fans in the bleachers began rhythmic stomping even before we started warming up. The local radio station prepared to broadcast the game for those who couldn't be there. I wondered if Charlene, who was back from her trip with her parents, would be able to listen.

Michael had painted an enormous purple and red (our school colors) banner that read, "Wildcats Shred the Trojans," which he hung off the railing of the upper bleachers. He sat beside Mom in the lower bleachers right next to third base. Mom had that brown and orange Navaho blanket, the one she brought to all my games, wrapped around her shoulders. During warm-ups, as I fielded grounders and tossed them to first, I could read the tension between them. Michael sat with his hands folded and dangling between his knees which he held humbly close together. He slouched a little as if to diminish himself. Roberta held the blanket around her like some kind of armor and wore her best "I don't give a shit" expression which was way too obvious to be effective. Both of them, I could tell, were trying very hard to let the game be the focus of the night, not each other. I also tried to let the game be the focus, not them and not Charlene's absence.

We won, of course. Not that it was an easy game, but I never questioned our winning. I felt as if everything rode on our victory. If we won that game, I had reasoned with myself, everything else would fall into place.

The fans swarmed onto the field. They picked up every last one of us on the team and passed us over their heads, shouting and singing the school song. Very corny. I didn't usually go in for that school spirit stuff, but it was fun for a few minutes.

I had plans, though, and needed to get out of there before the crowd thinned too much. I didn't want anyone to notice me leaving.

"Listen, Kathy," Mom yelled into my ear to be heard over the screaming fans. "Michael and I are going somewhere for coffee. I don't think we'll go over to Galluchio's. That okay with you?"

"Sure," I said, thinking *perfect*. "I'll see you later." I hardly had time to think about the significance of their going for coffee together I was so glad to have them leave. My knapsack was already packed. I'd go right now, straight from the game.

Though ten at night, it was hot, around seventy degrees, and I was still sweating from the game. I wore my uniform and walked as fast as I could. Mom and Michael running off together after the game made my getaway a cinch. Even so, I felt funny about them not going to Galluchio's with the rest of the team to celebrate. I mean, couldn't their stale old romance wait one more evening to get glued back together? After all we'd just won the State Championship! Yet, it *was* perfect because I wasn't going to go to Galluchio's myself, at least not for long, and would have had to come up with some fantastic excuse to get away, which I hadn't thought of yet. So I had no right to be so hurt. Still, I was.

Soon though, as I drew closer to the Desert View Motel, I forgot all about Mom and Michael. The anticipation of having Charlene in my hands, under my thighs, made me sweat more.

She was supposed to arrive first because she looked an easy eighteen, and I barely looked the fifteen I was. We chose the Desert View Motel, the last one on the highway out of town, about four miles from my house, two from hers. The place was a complete dump. We'd always wanted to go away together, to Alaska or Hawaii. A motel room, I thought, is a motel room. Tonight we could be near the Arctic Circle or at the base of a volcanic cone for all we'd know. I cared only that I would have Charlene to myself.

A car slowed and its driver asked if I wanted a ride. I almost took it, to get there faster, but I knew she wouldn't be there yet. I wasn't supposed to arrive first.

A few minutes later, there I was, standing in the small weedy courtyard of the Desert View Motel. I didn't know whether I should hang around and wait or try to check in. If I tried to check in and they didn't let me, we'd be stuck. If I hung around someone might see me, even call the police. A breeze scuttled across the courtyard. I felt exposed, spotlit, so I walked into the office. A middle-aged woman shuffled out of a doily- and afghan-draped living room adjacent to the office. She rubbed her hip as she walked, making sure that I knew I'd caused a woman with a bad hip to rise from the couch. She didn't speak and I saw that she considered asking for a room to be some sort of affront.

"Has a Cassandra Ogilvy checked in?" I asked. As I spoke, I caught the nauseous smell of hot wool, a mixture of the woman's dinner and the afghans. If I wasn't tasting Charlene's mouth on mine, smelling her lotion in my face, I'd have left in a second. Nothing short of Charlene could have kept me there.

The woman looked me over before checking her book. I felt conspicuous in my uniform. "No."

I pulled out thirty dollars and laid it on the counter. "I'd like a room."

She shook her head, as if I'd done something disgusting, and gripping her hip, bent to open a drawer where she kept cash. She took my money and handed me the key to number six.

The rug was gritty with dirt and the green walls smudged. The only light bulb that worked was in the bathroom. I pulled off the bedspread and wadded it up in a corner on the floor. It was made of that polyester material that gets lots of little balls on it. The sheets were not much better, full of cigarette burns, but at least they looked clean. I sat down and bounced on the springs, then closed my eyes and imagined the Pacific Ocean crashing against a beach outside the window. Possible, but Charlene would never buy it. I tried alpine slopes, a sharp slanting roof overhead, icicles pointing off the rafters right out the window. The sweat baking under my arms, running down the back of my neck, canceled out that one. I didn't mind that we were going to be right outside of town in a creepy motel, but I thought Charlene would.

I decided to clean up. The shower head was a good one and the cold water felt great. I let it leach the salt out of my hair first and then run down my front and back. I couldn't help touching myself, thinking about Charlene walking toward me now. She said she knew a back woods way to get here and would only have to come into sight of the main road when she ducked into the motel. She'd like it, I thought, if I watched for her out the window so she didn't have to go into the office and ask for me. We'd said midnight and it was eleven-thirty. So there was time to wait. And to shower. I thought of Charlene striding through the night heat, her big legs filling her jeans, her arms swinging wide the way they did. And I moved my fingers through the hair between my legs, let the water stream down my breasts. I thought of Charlene not wanting to be late, of her jogging a little, a light wetness forming on the back of her neck as I eased a finger up myself and then let it slide out and across my clit. I wanted her to taste like salt when she got here, I wanted Charlene to be flushed with anticipation. As I came, I saw Charlene's tongue, instead of my finger, sliding across me, easing into me. I fell back against the metal shower stall and moaned her name.

I heard a knock on the door. She was early! I quickly toweled myself dry and shouted, "Hold on one minute!" Suddenly I was shy and didn't want to open the door naked. I pulled on my jeans without underpants and found the clean white sweatshirt I'd brought in my knapsack. My hair a wet tangle, I pulled open the door, unable to control my enormous grin.

The proprietor of the motel stood at the door. She wore pea green stretch pants and her hair in curlers under a plastic cap. "Your change, you forgot it."

I took the money. She and I both knew the price of a room was twenty-eight dollars, there were signs everywhere, but when she hadn't offered me the two dollars back I figured she was accepting some kind of bribe. I wasn't sure what I would have bribed her for, silence maybe, but I'd let her keep it. Why had she changed her mind?

"You say you have a friend coming?"

I nodded. What was it to her?

"I'll send him along when he gets here."

"*Her* and *she*. Cassandra, remember?"

The woman looked me over once again.

"I'm renting a motel room, okay? Is it that big a deal?"

"I don't tolerate no drug dealing." Her eyes were keen, a metallic hazel. She could be as young as twenty-five, I realized, but she desperately wanted to be much older.

"I'll deal my drugs somewhere else then." I shut the door. I had to before I killed her for not being Charlene.

While I combed my hair I heard someone turning a key into the room next door. A bag was thrown against the wall, the TV clicked on.

I waited.

Being late was not unusual for Charlene. Who knew what she had to do to get away from her parents? Our plan was that she would go to bed at ten as usual, then slip out after they fell asleep. What if her father had to stay up late writing a sermon? She might not be able to even leave the house before midnight in which case she wouldn't get here for at least forty-five minutes.

The heat pushed in on my head. I couldn't get the window open so I opened the door. Between my room and number seven were two metal chairs and a man sat in one. "Who are you?"

"Ronald Sweisinger. You?"

"Laura Smith."

Ronald put out his hand. "Too hot for sleep, no?"

I fell into the chair next to him. I couldn't tolerate another second in that fetid motel room. This way Charlene could see me.

Ronald Sweisinger had a huge mouth with the largest and whitest teeth I'd ever seen. His hands were also very large and he combed them through his hair, over and over again, to keep the few long strands over his bald head.

"I used to be a carpet cleaner," he said. "Yourself?"

"I'm a high school student."

"I'm unemployed now. Out of work and out of a family. Wife left me."

I looked at him carefully, wondering if my room would be better.

"But I'm living it up tonight. A motel room. A bottle of rum. A six-pack of coke. Join me?"

"No thank you."

"Good girl. I didn't really want to be corrupting youth anyway. You hardly look old enough for high school. What are you doing in a dump like this? She your mother?" He pointed to the face pressed against the window of the room next to the office.

"No." I didn't want to talk about mothers. "I'm meeting a friend here."

Ronald leaned back and suddenly looked melancholy. "Savor it," he sighed. "Just savor it."

I tried to ignore him, but finally couldn't help asking, "Savor what?"

"Your sweetheart. Laura, you'll never again feel how you do now. Oh, god, do I remember my high school romance. Carla Remington. Homeliest little gal you ever laid eyes on, but what could I expect?" Ronald smiled apologetically and checked the hair covering his bald head.

"You're not bad looking," I said, surprising myself. I hated it when people didn't like the way they looked. Charlene always talked about looking horsey or being too fat.

"You're kind," Ronald said. He dropped a few pieces of ice from a bucket at his feet into a styrofoam cup, poured rum into the cup and then pulled open a coke and added it. "Carla had a head full of curly hair. Ever notice that all Carlas have curly hair?"

I knew one and she did.

"Carla and I were madly in love. We eloped, but her parents found us hitchhiking to Michigan and had the marriage annulled. I'd hoped that she'd gotten pregnant in our two days together, but she hadn't. So we were separated forever. I like to play a game with myself. I think of a certain juncture in my life and try to guess as accurately as possible how my life would have been different if I had done the thing I didn't do. There's a theory, you know, that every time you try to order something in the universe you simply set loose randomness somewhere else. For all I know, by keeping us apart Carla's parents might have started a civil war on another planet or caused the beginning of the greenhouse effect."

I smiled. I liked Ronald.

"Who's your young man, or do you mind my asking?"

"She's a young woman."

Ronald was quiet for a minute. Then he said, "Is it, well, a romantic relationship?"

"I guess so." I was not one for analyzing. Mom did enough of that for both of us.

"I never much understood that. You know, two gals or even two guys. That sort of thing is big out here, in the West I mean, isn't it?"

"Ronald, I don't know." I felt like a child just then and wanted him to treat me like one.

"I'm sorry," he said as if he understood.

Charlene was supposed to have been here an hour and a half ago. I worried. I knew she would want me to be inside hiding now. After all, it could be anything. Her father could be on his way with the sheriff. But what did I care? I had absolutely nothing to lose. Every last thing I wanted would meet me in this motel room—or would not.

Sometimes Ronald and I talked, sometimes we didn't. The minutes passed like the growth of a plant. If I watched, which I did most of the time, nothing changed. But now and then my mind broke loose and rose out over the desert like the moon, ethereal, light, and free. Then time grew and the hours passed.

At three in the morning, Ronald offered me some rum and coke again and I took it. The night was cool now, the moon had set, and the stars were dim. We sat silently for an hour, Ronald having caught me up on his entire life since Carla. I had told him the play-by-play account of the championship game that I had been preparing for Charlene. At four in the morning the phone in my room rang.

"Kathy. It's me."

My relief to hear her voice lasted only a second, then I was furious. "Charlene, where *are* you?"

"I can't get out," she whispered, her voice barely audible. "Tomorrow night. I'll try again."

"Charlene!"

She hung up.

I awoke the next day at noon and opened the door. A couple of cokes and half a bag of sour cream and onion potato chips sat next to our chairs from the night before. Ronald had left. I popped open a warm coke and slouched in one of the chairs. As I finished off the chips, I began to doubt everything that had happened between me and Charlene. Who was she, anyway? Maybe I'd made it all up so I didn't have to deal with Mom and Michael's breakup.

I knew that wasn't true. If nothing else, there had been that one moment at practice about a week before her mother found us in bed. I'd walked out to my position, paced off a few steps from third base. An afternoon breeze came up, and I was a little hungry—I always liked to play ball slightly hungry—and this peace came over me. It was like complete happiness, steadiness, all the squiggles in my head lying down and relaxed. It was a clean and spacious euphoria. I smiled at Charlene at short stop and she knew exactly what I was feeling.

"State of grace," she said.

"What?" I asked.

"It's a state of grace."

At six in the morning, after my second night in the Desert View Motel, I walked home. Charlene hadn't even called the second night. I felt like a dog. That loyal. That stupid.

The day was dusty and hazy. I scuffed along slowly wondering if Mom had sent out the police. I wondered if Michael would be there at the house. My eyes felt gritty and there was coke spilled on my sweatshirt. I wanted a shower, a good sleep, and then I wanted to toss the softball around a little.

The screen door to our place scraped the porch, as it always did, when I pulled it open. Mom and Michael jumped off the couch. Mom's eyes looked red and swollen. They both cried, "Kathy!" and fell all over me. For a few moments, as I clung onto Mom and Michael, I forgot all about Charlene. I finally cried.

That afternoon, after Mom called off the police and I slept, we barbecued some chicken and Michael made his special potato salad. I felt completely drained, both in the good relieved sense and in the bad empty sense. We didn't talk much, just sat on the porch together, the three of us, watching it grow dark and listening to the crickets.

I saw Charlene around town a few times that summer. She had graduated and gotten a job checking at Safeway. She ignored me and I never tried talking to her. I didn't really even want to talk to her anymore. Oh, she was still the same old Charlene, shouting jokes to the other checkers in Safeway, throwing groceries in the bags without caring whether she bruised avocados or squashed strawberries. But I saw that the authentic Charlene had sunk even deeper into her body and that she wasn't going to even try to coax her out.

It's not like I just let it all go easy, presto, I'm over her. I cried and sulked, took long soulful walks out to the ball field and lay on my back in left field for hours at a stretch. But I knew better than to look for the Charlene I loved—the Charlene who knew the meaning of grace—in the Charlene who checked groceries at Safeway and wouldn't speak to me. I'm not stupid. I realized pretty quickly that surviving Charlene was just another way of beginning my life.

Besides, I had learned that softball and sex were two separate things, and understanding that distinction was a far greater loss than losing Charlene. For the rest of my life I would be looking for the kind of sex that was synonymous with pine nuts and spring breezes, hardball and aching muscles. For love that was grass stains under a sky full of stars, the snap of my wrist and a hurtling softball, the taste of hard-won sweat. For the rest of my life, love would be letting go of Charlene.

SOLO

I STOOD ON THE RIM of a huge, perfectly formed bowl, deep with snow. I'd just skied over a pass that, according to my map, was 9,200 feet high. The peaks surrounding me were banked with snowfields that looked blue in the late afternoon High-Sierra light. Massive clouds, the color of pearls, swarmed around the peaks. And I knew exactly what I was—this being on skis in the marrow of wilderness—a human body and nothing more. That was one thing Elizabeth and I agreed on, even in the last couple years—that the goal is to reach that stripped down state where your cells know everything there is to know, where your feelings go so deep they become one simple force, where sorrow and joy become the same thing.

How I missed Elizabeth.

I cut the metal edges of my skis into the ice-crusted snow for balance and then reached into my pocket for a few yogurt peanuts. We'd always saved the yogurt peanuts to eat at the tops of passes, and nowhere else. Next, I checked to make sure the batteries in my avalanche beacon still had juice. What a joke, carrying a beacon on a solo trip. Who would pick up its high-frequency beeps if an avalanche buried me? I guess it was just habit.

Then I looked down into that steep bowl below me. Its snow pack fed a long drainage that in the spring would fan out into half a dozen streams. My destination was the bottom of that drainage. I planned to camp at High Meadow tonight and then ski out tomorrow morning. I scanned the slope for a safe route down. I figured it was about a five-hundred-foot drop.

"Yahooooo!" Elizabeth's voice hollered in my head. I could see her spirit lean forward with that open-mouthed grin of hers that looked more like a shout than a smile. She shoved her ski poles into the snow and flew off the mountain. Elizabeth would have taken what she called the crow's route, straight down. Her tight telemark turns would have made a long, neat squiggle in the snow all the way to the bottom of the bowl. In the meadow below she would glide to a luxurious stop, then purposely fall in a heap, exhausted from her ecstasy.

"Oh, Elizabeth," I said, missing her foolhardiness with a pain as sharp as this bitter wind. How I longed to lecture her right then: "Listen, girl, we've had over a foot of fresh snow in the last week. Got it? The snow pack is *weak*. Add to that the fact that this is a leeward slope on a gusty day."

By now she would have quit listening. Her face would be turned toward the valley and I'd know she was already flying, dead center in that rapture of hers.

And yet, I would go on with my lecture: "And look at that cornice!" I'd point to the one about ten yards below me right now.

"What cornice?" she might ask, because it really was a small one and nothing subtle ever figured into Elizabeth's world.

"Elizabeth," I spoke out loud now. "This is a prime avalanche slope in prime avalanche conditions."

I think my voice was an outside mantra for her, the droning

noise against which she took flight. My words of caution were her starting blocks. If she were here, this would have been her cue. Off she'd sail. I'd watch her back for a few moments and then realize that being stranded on a ridge top in the High Sierra in March, with a storm pending, was a greater risk than skiing an avalanche-prone slope. I'd be forced to follow.

The wind stormed over the pass, interrupting my thoughts and broadsiding me with so much force that I lost my balance and fell. I lay with my skis and legs tangled in the air above me, let my head fall back onto the snow, and watched the clouds. They'd lost their luster and were becoming swarthy. The feeling of knowledge in my cells disappeared and now I felt the opposite, as if I were all spirit, practically not here at all, like Elizabeth. How fast things changed at this elevation.

They found her car, of course. Who could miss it? Her bumper stickers were as loud as she was. This whole trip I'd been trying to imagine where her body might be. Deep in some crevasse. Buried in an avalanche. Or simply sitting in her camp somewhere, dead of exposure. I couldn't help wanting to believe that she had that shouting smile on her face, wherever she was, although even Elizabeth must have learned the meaning of fear in the moments before death. Or had she?

That they hadn't been able to find Elizabeth didn't surprise me in the least. She had always insisted on camping in the most remote places, hiking or skiing far off-trail, and changing her mind after the trip began so that even if we had told folks where we were going, it didn't matter. Perhaps in a month or two, when the snow melted, they would find her body.

Lying in the snow was a bad idea. I managed to get back on my feet and studied the slope again. The day wasn't getting any younger. My emotional state, as changeable as this mountain weather, cleared and the warmth colonized my cells again. I'd made this solo journey as a tribute to Elizabeth, and now I realized how this very moment, looking down at this perfect avalanche slope in the High Sierra, was the essence of Elizabeth. Here was her soul. She lived for this moment of risk. For the first time since we'd had our final falling out, I began to understand that I'd been as dependent on her for danger as she had been on me for safety.

Elizabeth, I think, knew this all along. She'd even tried to tell me that last trip of ours, but I'd been too angry to listen.

Elizabeth and I had been mountaineering partners, off and on, for almost twenty years. We began backpacking together when we were fifteen. I was the crazy one then, wild and daring, wanting to go farther, deeper, longer, faster, later or earlier. But over the years there was a shift. I grew more cautious and Elizabeth grew more reckless. There were several years in there, when her recklessness had caught up with but not yet overtaken mine, that we were perfect partners. We could choose a campsite and make route decisions almost without talking. We shared the implicit understanding that courting the mountains was our first commitment and working as a team got us closer to those peaks.

I noticed her impatience for the first time on a hiking trip in the Brooks Range of Alaska, just a few months after her mother died. She wanted to take a short-cut, bushwhack some ten miles across a spur where we could join our trail again and save thirty miles.

I pointed to the map. "Elizabeth, that's a cliff. And there aren't enough landmarks to ensure we'd find the trail. What's the hurry, anyway?"

"Don't use my name," she snapped.

"What?" I must have looked hurt.

"The way you use my name is patronizing. I can read the map. We can scramble up those rocks."

"You mean that vertical cliff."

"Oh, geez," she said but gave in to me. We had several similar encounters that trip, but I attributed her impatience to the recent death of her mother, nothing more.

Yet over the years I watched this impatience grow into a hunger she couldn't satisfy. She took too many inappropriate lovers—a coke head, a sixteen-year-old, several corporate execs—and wanted each of them body and soul. She embraced new spiritual teachers and practices every year, each time with fast conviction. And yet even as she acquired new lovers and gurus, she remained fiercely loyal to a few of her oldest friends, including her brother Nathan and me. Elizabeth searched for the heart of wilderness in every part of her life.

Back then I thought that if she would just slow down she could discover what it was she so badly needed. Now I think that she hungered only for this moment I faced. That in a strange, almost ghoulish way she got what she wanted—to see how far she could take a risk.

My choice now, to ski this prime avalanche slope or to turn around and ski out the three-day route I'd skied in on, was almost exactly like the one that precipitated Elizabeth's and my first all-out fight. We were circumnavigating Mount Adams in the state of Washington in the late spring. Near the end of the trip, we reached a torrential river gushing out of the foot of a glacier. We spent an entire day, at my insistence and to Elizabeth's disgust, searching for a safe crossing. We never found one.

"Our choice," Elizabeth finally pointed out, "is backtracking five days, being home late and not completing the circumnavigation, or jumping the river, being home in two days and completing the circumnavigation." Her gray eyes looked like nails.

"You missed one option," I added. "One of us jumps, lands in the river and is washed downstream. The other goes home to tell her family."

"Oh, shit." She looked up at Mount Adams as if appealing for understanding and I felt very small, cut out. I was in her way, had come between her and the mountain. And that, I knew, was the one sacrilege she wouldn't tolerate.

"Look," she deigned to explain. "Basically, there are two approaches to life. You can mire yourself in precautions as you endlessly try to outwit fate. Or, you can let her fly. There's risk either way. In the first scenario, you might—probably *will*—miss all that is good in life. In the second scenario, you get what you want, but you might not get it for as long as you want. Your choice."

I watched the chalky white glacial water as she hammered out her opinion. On either side of the river, a reddish moraine had built up, bereft of life. I longed for a forest then, the thick comfort of living things. I felt very alone with my cautious, fearful self. I also felt angry, used. I felt like that moraine, a pile of debris pushed aside by her forging glacier.

We did jump the stream, adrenaline carrying me across a much broader distance than my body could normally go. But nothing was ever the same between me and Elizabeth.

Another blast of icy wind, stronger still than the last one, blew me off my feet. I slid to within one yard of the cornice, my legs and skis once again a tangle. "Elizabeth!" I shouted. "I know you're out there! Quit pushing me, you wild woman."

Then, surprising myself I added, even louder still, "I love you!" In spite of everything, Elizabeth was as good as these mountains, this wild, stormy sky. She was part of my wilderness. But that didn't mean I had to be crazy, now that she was dead, and go against all common sense and ski this slope.

I had an idea. I'd have to check the map, but I thought that if I backtracked just to the other side of this pass, I could go out the south fork drainage and still only lose a day. I could hitchhike to my car from there. It was a good plan. I'd always told my friends that my coming home late meant nothing more than I'd used good sense and changed my route. I had plenty of food and warm clothing.

I got to my feet, without sliding over the lip of the cornice, and skied back to the top of the ridge. The hard wind died down suddenly and now a gentle breeze brushed my face. I stopped at the top to take one last look at the bowl before retreating down the back, gentle side of the pass.

"Yahooooo!" Once again, I saw her spirit fly over the cornice and down the slope.

I remembered the night of our final fight, a year ago, when we were marooned in our tent. I was lying on my stomach, cooking freeze-dried Szechwan chicken on the stove just outside the tent door, my sleeping bag pulled up to my shoulders. Outside, the snow fell thickly in tiny flakes. We'd been stuck in this camp for twenty-four hours already. Elizabeth had a date the following night and wanted to ski out in the morning regardless of the weather. "It's only fifteen miles," she'd said.

"Fifteen miles in a white-out."

She shrugged, "We've skied this route before."

"You'd risk your life for a date?" I challenged.

"Yeah," she grinned, "if it's hot enough. And this one is. I mean, I'm not talking about okay sex, this is, oh, how can I even explain to you . . ." She looked up to the ceiling of our tent, searching, as if the English language just didn't contain the words to make me understand.

"Elizabeth," I said calmly. "I know what hot sex is. And it's not worth dying in a blizzard for."

"Then," she said, snatching off her wool cap. Her short, honey-colored hair was mashed against her head. "Then you *don't* know what hot sex is."

"Oh, fuck you!" I yelled. I was so tired of her constant mocking. "You're a goddamn lunatic!" I managed to pull on my boots and squeeze out of the tent without knocking over the pot of Szechwan chicken cooking on the stove. I stomped around outside in the blizzard for a few moments, fuming.

When I started shaking violently with cold, I returned. She had a novel propped on one knee and the last of our yogurt peanuts in a plastic bag between her legs. The chicken bubbled away, most of the liquid boiled off. She wolfed down the yogurt peanuts one after another, munching loudly.

"What are you doing?" My voice was dry and accusing. "Those peanuts are for the pass tomorrow."

"I'm feeding the lunatic," she answered softly, faking innocence. "She's hungry." A bit of chewed up yogurt peanut spewed out of her mouth as she spoke. She held the bag out to me. "I think your lunatic may be hungry, too. Want some?"

"Oh, fuck you," I said again. And we were silent the rest of the evening. I lay awake all night reading short stories and looking forward to being rid of Elizabeth at the end of this journey.

By the next morning the sky had cleared and we skied out, Elizabeth happy to be heading back to the Bay Area in time for her hot date. Me, bitter. It was the last trip we took together. She called me occasionally after that, but neither of us suggested any trips. I went with other friends, she went alone. I dreaded the day when she would see our impasse as yet another unexplored territory she must venture into.

I did find some satisfaction in the fact that she didn't take another partner. Yet, in a way, I was even more jealous that she went solo, that she'd stretched to a place I didn't think I could stretch to.

When her brother called me two months ago to ask if I'd heard from Elizabeth, I knew instantly. He figured maybe an impromptu trip to L.A. Or that she was camped out at some new lover's apartment. "Nathan," I told him. "I don't think so." He waited silently for my explanation and I could tell from his breathing that he knew too. I said, "She'd mentioned a trip in the Trinity Alps last time I talked to her."

"Who should I call?" Nathan asked dully. I hung up and went over to his apartment. We called the Forest Service and they located her car within five hours. They gave up looking for her body after a week.

For a long time, all I could think was that I had been right and she had been wrong. She was dead, and still I wished I could continue our dispute, find some way of telling her "I told you so." Now, as I turned my back on the bowl, deep with snow, preparing to retreat back down the safe side of the pass, I realized just how great my jealousy had been. She was right. My lunatic *was* hungry.

Suddenly, I turned around again and faced the steep bowl. A pillow of fog nestled in the trees far below. Somewhere beyond was my car.

I dug my poles into the snow. I pushed slowly at first and then shoved off hard. I sailed out, directly over the lip of that cornice and landed squarely on my skis several feet below. I shot downhill, taking the crow's route, straight down. I wasn't a particularly good downhill skier, I'd never learned telemark turns, so I skied a straight, seemingly vertical line, amazed that I didn't fall. My feet vibrated as they stroked the long slope. My legs felt like springs, supple and responsive. My head roared. Everything was a white blur. I'd never skied so fast in my life.

Then I heard it. A bellowing that drowned out the rush of wind in my ears. I felt the entire mountain thundering under my feet. In the next split second, I saw powder snow billowing up fifty feet in the air. So this was it, I thought, feeling a strange, dead center calm. No one skied faster than a slab avalanche. And yet, as if I could, I crouched down lower, held my poles close to my body, allowed my legs to be even more elastic, and concentrated on the width between my skis.

Then the avalanche overtook me, careening down the slope to my right, missing me by about ten yards. The roar was deafening and the cloud of snow blinded me, but still I skied.

Elizabeth, I thought, perverse in the coolness of my mind, never raced an avalanche down a slope.

I came crashing into the flats of the meadow below the bowl and plunged into the snow, face first. Sharp pain splintered up my nose, across my jaw. I rolled over on my side and gingerly wiped the snow off my face with a wet mitten, touching my cheekbone and forehead. Nothing seemed to be broken, just mashed. I blinked hard to clear my eyes, and finally saw the wreckage of the avalanche to my right; masses of snow that moments ago were as fluid as water and now as set as concrete. I could have been locked in that pile of snow, my beacon transmitting tiny beeps for some chance stranger to pick up. They would have had about thirty minutes, if I was lucky, to locate and dig me out. I stared and stared at that icy rubble as awed as if it were the remains of a ancient temple.

"Oh, god," I whispered.

My arms and legs felt paralyzed, but slowly I was able to move each limb, bending and straightening until it regained feeling. I rolled over in the snow and tried to get to my feet, but didn't yet have the strength.

I sensed Elizabeth nearby. "Did you see me?" I asked, still whispering.

Finally I wept, and as I did I thought I heard her laughing, that hard, wild woman laughter of hers. Until I realized it was my own laughter, in concert with my tears, shaking the very centers of my cells, wringing the sorrow out of my pores.

SEX IS AN ANCIENT PRACTICE

TWO ADORABLE YOUNG THINGS, they couldn't have been more than twenty-five, sat down at a table near mine in the Hipper Than Thou Cafe. The one with the chartreuse flattop grazed over me with her eyes, making me feel like a blank wall. She was that uninterested. The one with the shredded T-shirt smirked, "Shit, I'm glad I wasn't born into the plaid flannel shirt, take-back-the-night era."

Had I inspired this comment?

Chartreuse flattop shook her head with pity at my whole generation. "Puritans," she spat. "How can they live without sex?"

"Oh, you know," Shredded T-shirt answered, "they do the I-do-you/you-do-me routine biannually."

Uproarious laughter from the young ones.

In the discussion that followed it became clear that these women believed they had invented a number of new ways to get off unknown to all the homo Homo sapiens in our three million years on earth before these two gals showed up.

I tried to keep an open (and voyeuristic) mind and listened carefully to their stories of sexual discovery. Their little sexual tête-à-tête soon launched them into a discussion of radical politics, this being another area, like hot sex, in which their generation had made astounding breakthroughs.

"Can you believe Alicia kissed that *separatist* at the kiss-in on Thursday?"

"Oh, I believe it! I saw her kiss a woman in a business suit and pumps at the last one."

"Nooo." Chartreuse flattop seemed to *taste* this dirt.

"Yep. I don't even know what she's doing at the kiss-ins."

"She's *soooo* mainstream."

"Retro even," Shredded T-shirt added.

"You know, I was talking to Jeff and Rocky the other day. We thought we should sever our focus group from the organization. You know, just be a renegade group of queer radicals." The idea turned on Chartreuse flattop so much she squirmed cutely in her chair. I think it was the word "renegade."

Shredded T-shirt rushed to agree. "Just hearing the others talk about all that drivel they read drives me crazy."

The girls began assaulting the publications they didn't read—*Down and Out* (for depressed queers), *Out/Sider* (for alienated queers), *Scream Out* (for frustrated queers), *Out/Back* (for wilderness queers), *Spit It Out* (for timid queers), and *Out/Cry* (for angry queers)—and lauding the one they did read—*Fuck!* That got them going on how, when they really thought about it, even the members of their own focus group, even Jeff and Rocky, didn't quite grasp the full political import of universally-expressed sexuality. They proudly reviewed (*again*) their own sexual versatility, this time mentioning pet birds, a number of possibilities for sand paper, and utilizing the vibrating butt of a power saw.

I couldn't stand it any longer. I set down my triple decaf cappuccino, grabbed one of the girls by the frayed collar of her T-shirt, took the other by the crown of her chartreuse flattop, and pulled them to their feet.

"What the fuck!" one screamed.

"Let go of me, you—" the other began.

I dropped them both in the empty chairs at my own table and began. "Let's start with 1960. Girls, ten years before you were even thought of, my basketball coach caught me on my knees in the shower room, my best friend Joella straddling my face. My head and shoulders were lost up under her knee-length skirt, so that just my bare legs, bunched up bobby sox and saddle shoes were showing. Naturally, in that position I didn't see Coach come in. I thought Joella was coming when I heard her quick intake of breath, but then I heard Coach's voice. She had been in the army and often used military commands. I heard her say, in a shaky, emotion-laden voice, 'At ease.' By the time I managed to emerge from under Joella's skirt, Coach was already gone.

"Let your imaginations suck on that one for a while as I skip a few years ahead to 1965. Perhaps your het parents were courting while I was immersed in free love, sleeping with anything that moved, as you like to say. (Hell, maybe I even slept with one of your parents.) I soon discovered though that certain moving things thrilled me more than others: in particular, girls in bubble hair-dos, miniskirts, fishnet stockings, and shiny white plastic go-go boots. I'll never forget that one civil rights march where Bobbi Sue and I made it behind a warehouse building on Front Street and I didn't learn until late that evening, when I looked in a mirror, that she'd smeared her frosty white lipstick all over my face and neck. And she'd made such a scene about my mussing her bubble do and tearing her poorboy sweater!

"Let's do 1970. Perhaps the very day you slipped from the womb was the same day I did acid with my two best girlfriends at the beach. After spending the early hours debating fine political fractures, we marveled at how you could soak dried apricots in water and come out with something strikingly similar to certain female anatomy. Licking these apricots only whetted our appetites for the real thing, so we indulged ourselves. Oh, sure, there were lots of families at the beach that day. If my memory serves me a park cop even watched us for a while but was too afraid, or too fascinated, to approach us. The sand undulated beneath us, the whole beach became our water bed, and the rest . . . I forget.

"Okay, so my generation lost a few years in the late sixties, early seventies, but we snapped to by 1975. You must have been in preschool, sweethearts, slobbering on graham crackers and pouring cartons of milk down your flat fronts, when I shaved my head (just like yours today) and marched with the rest of the girls for every kind of right you can imagine. Our ideas from back then may seem retro to you now, but you're standing on the strong backs of those ideas, including separatism.

"As for sex, the Penetration Debates were raging while our shopping carts were piled high with carrots and cucumbers. Sure, we were all vegetarians, but no one can eat *that* much roughage.

"By 1980, when you were tackling long division, I was sleeping with all four of my roommates (simultaneously) and plotting to overthrow the government. The S/M Debates flared up, but like the Penetration Debates, these were for girls who got off on arguing in magazines. Don't be fooled—more gals were doing what they wanted with their bodies than our literature has ever let on.

"In 1985 I bet you went on your first date. Maybe it was even with a girl. Maybe your high school had a gay and lesbian club! That's beautiful. By then I had come to realize that whatever I did with my body—vanilla, chocolate or strawberry—was my own damn business, so I won't even tell you what I was into."

I took a deep breath and looked at their attentive, if a little shell-shocked, faces. "So listen, I didn't mean to blast you or anything. I just wanted you to know that sex is an ancient practice. I may wear plaid flannel shirts, I may have graying hair, maybe I was even a separatist once, but even we older lesbians have been having sex, blockbuster sex, *frequently*, since before you explained to us how to do it."

The humbled looks on their faces softened me, so I added, "But hey, I'm open to new ideas. About that power saw, what did you say you could do with it?"

THE PASS

BABY! BABY! Oh, baby!" my coach shouted, gripping my shoulders. Johnny practically yanked me off my bike seconds after I'd crossed the finish line.

"Easy, man, hey, easy," I protested as he crushed me against his chest in his version of a hug. Johnny slopped a big wet one right on my mouth.

"Johnny . . ." I muttered, shaking his mania off me. Sure, I could understand his ecstacy. His team just took first place in the Rocky Mountain Classic, a 50-mile road race in Wyoming. I mean, we weren't a bigshot team like Kahlua or TGIF. No one expected a team from an obscure bike shop in Berkeley to take first place.

Even so, the finish line meant little to me right then. I was still savoring what had happened up on Snow Pass.

I watched Johnny tackle Julie and Danielle, my teammates as well as my lover of five years and affair of six months, respectively. After Johnny galloped off to greet our fourth teammate, Kelly, Danielle turned on me. "What happened?"

"What do you mean?" I knew exactly what she meant. At the end of the race, I'd blocked in the final sprint for Kelly, rather than

Danielle, to get into the final sprint and take first place.

"The finish line?" Danielle swung her long black ponytail back and forth across her shoulders in that way she had of trying to look oh-so-relaxed. She fingered the two gold chains glinting at her neck. I think my fascination with her centered on the fact that she was even more femme than me.

"We took first place," Julie defended me to Danielle. "It doesn't matter who she blocked for." Julie stood with her fists on her hips, looking short and sturdy next to wispy Danielle. I used to love the way Julie's face, framed by that short blond hair, looked blunt with sincerity as she argued a point, but now Julie's earnestness put me off. It was overdone, an accessory, like Danielle's gold chains. In fact, it was a lie. Julie was just as angry as Danielle at what happened between me and Kelly in this race.

"We had a strategy," Danielle argued. "You had no idea if Kelly could sprint. This was her first race with us. The whole purpose of strategies . . . ."

"Yeah," I muttered and stopped listening. I watched Kelly over by the finish line as some guys pressed an obscenely gaudy trophy into her arms. Johnny stood close by, hiccupping his wolfish laughter. Kelly looked as if she were searching for someone in the crowd. I caught her eye. She didn't smile, but she got that focussed look of hers, as if she were filled with intent. I could tell that she too felt something much bigger than that trophy in her arms. She'd taken off her helmet and her hair was slick with sweat. Her big legs glistened with sweat as well. Though she was a good twenty yards away, I felt Kelly's presence as powerfully as if she were occupying every cavity in my body. I forced myself to turn my back. I didn't need to posture or rush. I had all afternoon and evening. More, if it took more.

"See you in a bit," I told Danielle and Julie and walked off pushing my bike. Most of the racers and spectators were heading for the barbecue, but I wanted a moment alone. A good distance away from the food tables I found a small grove of aspens. I propped my bike against a tree and lay down on my back in the spotted sunlight. The leaves above me were an iridescent yellow with auras of orange and red. Beyond the leaves I could see the steel gray mountains and the sky so dense with blue you could stab it with a fork. I felt the sweat on my body drying into a sandy film. I licked the corner of my mouth and tasted it, gritty and salty. Every muscle in my body felt like liquid bliss. If just thinking about that woman made me feel like this, what would touching her be like? I closed my eyes, praying that Johnny, Danielle, and Julie would leave me alone for at least five minutes.

Until about three hours ago, at the beginning of the hill leading up to Snow Pass, I'd barely acknowledged that Kelly had joined the team a few weeks ago. I guess I was too enmeshed in the sticky triangle with Julie and Danielle. It shouldn't have been sticky. Julie, who called herself a socialist, always said that, and I quote, "jealousy is simply a residual emotion left over from the corruption of capitalism." We'd both had affairs and jealousy had never played a part. Something about Danielle, though, really set Julie off. I think it was her corporate job. She was a buyer for Macy's. Danielle liked to tell Julie, "Competition is everything." To me, when Julie wasn't around, she would add that Julie would only be a good bike racer, never great, because she always compromised the spirit of competition. I was tired of being in the crossfire of their ideologies. And I wondered if either of them could ever understand what had happened on Snow Pass.

As the pack approached the bottom of the hill I was a lot more tired than I should have been. Sweat drenched my jersey. Sharp pains traveled from my neck across my right shoulder. That hill was eight miles long and the pack was already moving pretty fast. Yet, as the strongest hill climber on the team, in spite of my being the oldest at thirty-eight, I was supposed to lead an attack at the start of the hill.

Trying to ignore my fatigue and pain, I rose out of the saddle and pumped to the front of the pack and then out in front. At first I thought the whole pack was coming with me, but I guess most of the riders figured an attack so early in the climb was foolish. We made a strong break with Julie, Danielle, Kelly, two riders from a Denver team, as well as an independent rider, coming along.

"Excellent," Kelly growled after climbing for a mile. "Perfect breakaway." She pulled in front of me so I could draft her for a while.

I needed the encouragement. The breakaway effort nearly killed me and I wasn't recovering quickly. It was pretty spectacular that all four of us on the Berkeley team broke away together, no one stranded back in the pack.

As we continued up the mountain pass in a paceline of seven riders, I realized that one thing I liked about bike racing was how cooperating with your competition is an essential part of the strategy. This was a good group. Everyone except for Danielle, who was saving herself for the sprint at the finish line, was willing to work, taking her turn pulling at the front then falling back to draft and "rest."

Despite our successful escape from the pack and the smooth work of my teammates, I felt weaker and weaker. I couldn't get enough oxygen into my lungs. My legs felt like they were going to burst apart. When it was my turn at the front I just couldn't keep the pace. I knew I was hitting the wall in a very serious way.

The girls from Denver and the independent rider took advantage of my failing strength and worked together to break away from us.

"We've got to go with them," Danielle ordered. I watched their three behinds swinging from side to side as they moved up the hill ahead of us. Danielle snarled, "Come on, *jam*."

"You can do it," Julie urged me. "We can bridge up if you try. They're not that far out front."

"I can't," I gasped. I knew this was not a phrase athletes use. Ever. But it was true. I was bonking big time.

"I don't mean you," Danielle said to me. Which made me think immediately of how she was twenty-five to my thirty-eight.

"Then who *do* you mean?" Kelly, who was taking a pull at the front with me right behind her, asked. I felt a surge of emotion for her. It was as if I noticed her, really noticed her, for the first time.

Danielle, knowing that she couldn't bridge up to the other riders alone and probably not wanting to ask Julie to go with her, muttered, "There goes the race."

"They're not going to be able to hold that pace," Kelly shouted from the front of the paceline to Danielle at the back. "Don't worry about them." In a lower voice, just to me, she said, "How come Danielle never takes a pull at the front?"

Julie, who rode right behind me, heard the question and smirked, "Because she's a prima donna."

"Don't start," I found the breath to say.

"What?" Danielle yelled from the back of the paceline.

Luckily, I couldn't answer. The wall felt grayer and thicker and harder than it ever had before. My gut was heaving up into my throat with every revolution. I felt as if a massive steel weight rested on my shoulders.

"Danielle!" Kelly called back. "Take your turn at the front."

"Since when is she calling the shots?" Danielle called up and I knew she was asking me.

"Take a pull," I told Danielle. "We need help."

"It's about time," Julie mumbled as Danielle rode past us on her way to the front of the paceline.

I was surprised that Danielle complied. She espoused "team play" all the time, whether she was talking about selling clothes or having sex, but in cycling team play meant our catering to her role as finish line sprinter. She threatened me as she went by, "I just hope I have it in me to sprint at the end."

"You're climbing up to Snow Pass now," Kelly said, sliding in behind Danielle. "Think about sprinting to the finish line in twenty miles. If you get there."

Kelly's voice felt good. I couldn't tell what it was, but it had to do with massaging the wall instead of beating it, like Julie and Danielle's voices seemed to do. Watching her ride helped me too. I'd never seen a smoother cyclist. Her muscles flowed with each pedal stroke. She could tell how badly I was struggling and counseled me in a low voice, "Let go of your mind. You don't need it. Don't think. Your legs will do all the work."

That's when the wall in front of me metamorphosed and I realized it was my whole life in my face, like a blockade. Two girlfriends, two part-time jobs, the eternal mess of my apartment . . . . I was sick of it all. If I was going to make it up this hill something had to go. I cut out Danielle. Maybe this one-minute manager routine worked on the job, but applied to me it was a drag. Julie was right: Danielle's oh-so-femme corporate number was definitely expendable.

I breathed deeply and heard Kelly say, "That a girl. A few more miles."

"Sure," I said. Deleting one girlfriend helped, but was only a beginning.

"We've got to pick up the pace," Danielle prodded. She'd slipped rather quickly back into the fold and Julie now led us up the hill.

No one answered her. Something cruel in me enjoyed knowing

that I'd broken up with her and she didn't even know about it.

Kelly said, just to me, "I don't know, but I think this might be the ideal pace. I have a hunch that we'll bridge up to those others without trying. And we'll be fresher."

I didn't have the strength to tell her that fresh, fresher, and freshest were relative terms, none of which applied to me.

To take my mind off the hill, I concentrated on each muscle in Kelly's legs, one at a time. She reminded me of an elk I'd once seen running in a Canadian forest. The elk had the most magnificent set of antlers which it negotiated through the tree branches and even under fallen logs with complete grace and precision, clearing obstacles by half an inch but never knocking its antlers.

Kelly's legs, and the memory of that elk, made me consider editing Julie out of my life along with Danielle. The thought felt razor-sharp and clear. As I thought it, the structure of the wall shimmered as if it were deconstructing. Then I wavered, feeling the loss, of Julie or the wall, I wasn't sure which. My breathing became ragged and my shoulders suddenly ached even worse. Again I thought of that elk and how Kelly reminded me of it and *that* made me think about how there had never been passion, real passion, between Julie and me, in all our five years together. We used to believe that neither of us ever got jealous of the other's affairs because of our superior ability to deal with nonmonogamy. In truth, our lack of jealousy was probably more a sign that our love wasn't the kind you can cut yourself on.

I felt something like an explosion in my head. The wall melted away in its heat. I reached a blank place, but blank in the sense of remembering, not forgetting. Blank and utterly peaceful. I realized how badly I had been missing myself.

A fluid strength took residence in my body. I pulled to the front of the paceline to haul us the last mile to the top of the pass. Now Kelly drafted me and I could hear her breathing, even, full and deep. I could feel her front wheel inches behind my back wheel. She hadn't said more than a few sentences to me in all the time I'd known her, but the way her body worked told me plenty.

As we drew near the top of the pass I shifted up a gear to push our pace. My legs and mind were free now. I could do anything. I jammed up that hill with Kelly breathing on my back, and I knew all that mattered was the taste and texture of this blue sky. The flow of sweat off my head. The rolling muscles in my back. I gulped the Rocky Mountain air as if it had nourishment.

As we crested the top of the pass, I sat up in my saddle for a moment and whooped, "Yeah, *baby*!"

Julie warned, "Take it easy," and I knew she meant to check the joy in me as if it were decadent.

"Take it easy?" Danielle snarled. "Now's the time to *hit it.*"

Kelly shifted into her biggest gear and pulled in front of me. We soared over the top of the pass and began down the other side. Like hers, my chin nearly rested on my handlebars and we moved as one machine flying down the hill. I didn't care anymore what Julie or Danielle had to say. I didn't care anything about the race or the finish line. All I cared about was the relief I felt in having one focus, to ride with Kelly.

On either side of us the late afternoon sun painted angular shapes onto the rocky cliffs. We flew into patches of shade, where I thrilled at riding nearly blind, then sped out into the bright sunshine again.

"There's a hairpin turn at the bottom of the hill!" Julie screamed and I was surprised that she and Danielle had kept up with Kelly and me. "Slow down," she yelled.

Her words were lost in the rush of wind in our ears. I'm sure I was the only one who heard her and I didn't answer.

A moment later the independent and the two Denver riders came into sight ahead of us, then disappeared around the bend.

"Attack on the turn," Kelly shouted back to me. Without braking even a little, I tilted my bike toward the apex of the curve and put all my weight on my outside foot. Kelly and I shot right through the other riders.

It was then, as we screamed into that hairpin turn and sailed through the other racers, that I grasped the one hard knot of truth I'd been missing. I was a wild animal then, the bicycle was my set of antlers, and I knew down to a fraction of an inch how to maneuver through that turn at this wild speed.

I also knew, right there at the apex of the turn, that I had to have Kelly. I wanted her because I knew that when I touched her I would relive screaming through this hairpin turn, because I knew that she would feel excruciatingly necessary, like the hard knot itself.

I heard Johnny shout, "There she is!"

Cracking open an eye, I saw him corralling Julie and Danielle over to my place under the aspens. He held up a paper plate piled high with chicken, fruit, and pasta salad. "I got ya some eats!" Poor Johnny, I thought. He knew everything there was to know about cycling and nothing about the dyke subtext, the very soul of competition, that drove every race.

Danielle's cleats tapped along on the cement pathway just as I imagined her high heels did in the management hallways of Macy's. Julie looked a little confused and I figured that she was constructing her case against me.

I had an awful lot of explaining to do. I wished I could have stood up and said, "Look, I decided during the race that I want to break up with both of you, and the reason I blocked for Kelly at the finish line, rather than for you, Danielle, was because, well, I wanted to."

A thread of courtesy kept me from giving that speech. Instead, I pretended to doze.

"We're having a team meeting. Do you think you could regain consciousness for a few minutes?" Danielle wanted to know.

"Sure." I rolled over on my side and propped up on an elbow. Johnny placed the plate of food on the ground in front of me.

Then I saw both Julie and Danielle glaring at something behind me. I looked over my shoulder and saw Kelly approaching with a plate of food in one hand. She cradled the enormous trophy with her other arm.

"Hi," I said, my voice full of her. That thread of courtesy snapped and I caressed Kelly with my eyes right there in front of everyone.

Not that I was in a hurry, *au contraire*, but I wasn't about to waste another moment of my life either.

"Hi," Kelly answered after a long pause. Then she smiled, her whole face crunching up in a look of complete happiness. I think I moaned a little.

"So Johnny wants to know," Julie said flatly, "how Kelly got into the sprinter's position."

Everyone looked at me.

"I mean, I have no problem with it!" Johnny bellowed, still grinning widely. "First place is first place. I just want to know how you all rode the race."

I sat up suddenly, feeling delirious. "Hey! I've had an insight." I said, "When you think about it, it's pretty strange we have these big knobs, called heads, bobbing around on the tops of our bodies. I mean heads are just very densely packed masses of nerve cells. No wonder we all get so twisted up mentally. I know we have nerve cells all over, but the great majority of them are way up in our heads. Wouldn't it make a lot more sense if those nerve cells—our intelligence—were spread evenly throughout our whole bodies? Julie, in your terms it would be a kind of redistribution of the wealth. In yours, Danielle, let's just call it diversification."

I let that sink in and then said more quietly, "What happened in the crucial moments of this race is that Kelly and I managed to psychically spread our nerve cells throughout our bodies so that our bodies were able to make all the decisions. Does that make sense?"

I looked at Kelly. She looked as if she were about to kiss me, and I was flooded with unbearably intense desire.

"No it doesn't," Danielle said. When I looked over at her she was smirking at Julie. Julie's face relaxed and she smiled at Danielle. Ah, the subtle beginning of an alliance. It was inevitable really. In the course of one race I'd transformed a triangle, with all its stagnant tension, into a square. Triangles can stay in place forever, but squares quickly break off into pairs.

"The problem with you two," I said to Julie and Danielle, "is that you both live too much in your heads."

I enjoyed the silence I'd shocked them into. I glanced at Johnny and he looked thoroughly confused. Kelly remained quiet and still.

I picked up a chicken leg and teethed off the meat. When the bone was clean, I cracked it in two and began sucking out the marrow. I wasn't sure if this would impress or disgust Kelly, but I didn't feel very cautious today. I needed a woman who could handle a marrow-sucking, hill-jamming, hard-cycling femme. Take it or leave it. I put down the hollowed-out chicken bone, wiped my mouth on a napkin, and smiled at Kelly. She cracked the chicken bone on her own plate, put it to her mouth, and started sucking out the marrow.

"I can't believe this," Danielle said. She got to her feet. "Let's go."

Johnny looked downright spooked. Maybe I was acting even more deranged than I felt. Usually I'm a nice person. You know, considerate of other people's feelings. He said, "Yeah, well, maybe we all need to rest a little before rehashing the race."

He, Danielle and Julie were all standing now, ready to leave. The light was beginning to fail. The leaves of the aspens deepened to a rich mustard color. It began to get a little chilly and still I didn't want to move. I was afraid that if I did the nerve cells would all rush back into my head.

Johnny and Danielle began walking back to the van. Julie waited. She looked hurt and I felt a spasm of guilt. She said, "What's wrong with you? Come *on.*"

I answered, "I think I'll ride my bike back to the motel."

"In the dark," she snapped. "Twenty miles."

"Yeah," I said. "In the dark. Twenty miles."

Julie didn't bother asking if Kelly was coming. I watched her turn her back and head for the van. Briefly I wondered why I felt so detached, so careless with her feelings. My worries only lasted a millisecond. The earthy smell of the ground beneath me and the papery rustle of the alder leaves above returned me to the present. I turned to Kelly. Her face looked like a racer, intent and specific.

"That was only the beginning," she said, and I knew she was talking about what happened on both sides of the pass. She leaned forward and untied the laces of my cleats. Her fingers brushed my ankles, searing the skin as hotly as if she'd touched my most sensitive places.

Then someone shouted her name. She laughed and looked over her shoulder at the couple of dozen racers, spectators, and reporters gathered around the food tables.

"Your public is waiting for you," I said.

She retied my cleats and then ran her hands up my leg. "Then maybe I'd better leave your clothes on until I finish talking to the reporters."

"I'm in no rush," I told her. "I'll be right here."

I watched her walk toward the crowd. There was no swagger to her movement, no butch announcements, though she was as beautifully butch as I could hope for. I closed my eyes, listening to the alder leaves and thinking that the fourth dimension had dropped out altogether up there on Snow Pass. I could wait a lifetime for this woman and feel as if I hadn't missed a thing.

UNDER THE CABAÑA

DEBBIE TOLD three travel agents that she wanted an island without a nightlife. None believed her. They suggested resorts that were known for attracting only professionals, for not being sleazy, or, as one agent claimed, for having the best-looking clientele in the Caribbean.

They didn't understand. Debbie meant *no* nightlife. Zip. She didn't want to meet men without Suz. She'd have to figure out a whole new dating strategy, but that would be later. This week, for once in her life, she was going to be alone. She'd never done that. For ten years, since they met in their sophomore year at the University of Oklahoma, she and Suz had taken all their vacations together.

Debbie finally found a travel agent who specialized in diving trips. She didn't want to dive, but this woman took her at her word and booked her on the north end of Grand Cayman Island, at a diving hangout called Cayman Kai Resort. The agent promised she'd find plenty of solitude. Debbie noticed on the map that Grand Cayman was just one island over from Jamaica where Suz and Gregory would be honeymooning that same week. The idea made her feel vaguely perverse, like someone who stands outside the door of a roommate having sex. She didn't tell Suz she'd planned a Caribbean vacation for herself because she didn't want Suz to feel sorry for her, or worse, to think that she was somehow trying to butt in.

After she drove the newlywed couple to the Tulsa airport and left them off in front of the TWA ticket counter, Debbie circled around to long-term parking and pulled the Buick, frosted with shaving cream and trailing tin cans, into a space. She kicked the cans under the car and walked empty-handed to the terminal. She'd brought her bag yesterday morning, before the wedding rehearsal, and stowed it in a locker.

Debbie arrived on Grand Cayman just two hours after Suz and Gregory landed on Jamaica.

Rum Point, the finger of island on which Cayman Kai Resort was situated, was deserted and it was pouring rain. The "resort" was a jumble of small cabins, a modest restaurant, and one cabaña on the beach. The belt of sand stretched out in either direction, long and wet and empty. The sea was an angry gray and choppy. Hardly the velvet blue she remembered from other Caribbean trips. This water looked more like sharks than angelfish.

Debbie's cabin was just twenty yards from the water. She jammed the key in the lock, her eyes filling with tears. What had she been thinking when she planned this trip?

The idea of a tropical week alone had thrilled her all the way up to the time of the wedding. It had given her the kind of strength that only secrets can give. Suz would have her wedding, and Debbie would have coconuts, palm trees, a sea as soft and blue as deep twilight. And her own thoughts, nothing more, for an entire week.

But during the wedding, as she stood in the mango-hued maid of honor gown she'd helped Suz pick out, she panicked. They had always traveled together. It had been the best part of every year. She realized that a week alone wasn't going to feel like a week with herself but instead a week without Suz. Why did this wedding feel as if it were erasing years of fun? Debbie wanted to shake Suz and ask, "What about that time we drank a whole bottle of tequila on that beach in Acapulco and slept all night in the sand? Or the time we danced naked to Tina Turner blaring full volume in my apartment—with the shades up—and the landlady evicted me the next day? Or other times, like when I held you and sobbed with you when you lost your mother?"

Her jealousy was childish, of course, she thought as she finally got the door open and stepped into her cabin. This rain wouldn't last and her sadness would disappear with it. By evening, the skies would clear and she'd plunge into the sea for her first swim of the week. Debbie unpacked her things, trying to ignore the rain banging on the roof. She looked for the TV, hoping it would overpower the noise, but didn't find one.

After a quick shower, Debbie changed into shorts and a T-shirt and went for a walk in the rain. Coconuts, blown in from the storm, floated in the surf, and she found two conch shells lying on the beach. One shell was sand encrusted, but the other was polished smooth, its insides orangy-pink. She bent down to run her finger along the silky inner shell. When the sun came out, this place would be paradise. Debbie returned to her cabin and spent the rest of the afternoon reading a novel. She wondered if it were raining on Jamaica.

That night Debbie had dinner alone in the restaurant. Three women sat laughing and talking at the bar. Other than that, there was only one other person in the restaurant, a man eating alone. Debbie wished he wouldn't keep glancing at her.

Meeting men had never been a problem for Debbie. She had the kind of cautious good looks lots of men like: long, bouncy brown hair, easy features and green eyes, a withdrawn chin that made her look vulnerable. She was pretty but not threateningly beautiful. She thought that Suz was ten times cuter with her big dimples and perennially-flushed cheeks, even if she was a bit chunky and tended to wear her neck-length blond hair in a stubby pony-tail rather than blow-dried like the stylist had shown her.

Debbie had finished her salad and taken her first bite of snapper baked in coconut milk when the man came over and politely asked if he might join her. Debbie's first thought was, oh, this is already a good story for Suz. Then she realized she wouldn't be able to tell Suz without confessing to having taken this trip, which she couldn't do because of the part that felt voyeuristic, like she'd come here just to be one island over in the same sea as Suz and Gregory.

"Sure," Debbie said, feeling suddenly like she wanted to spite Suz. The man bounded back to his table, grasped his plate of fish, rice and beans, and returned.

"Bradley," he said, extending his hand across the table after he'd seated himself. He had wiry black hair, cut short, a neat mustache, big green eyes, and pleasingly generous cheeks.

"I'm Debbie," she said. "I teach third grade." What a dumb thing to say. She felt exposed without Suz at her side. Suz knew how to keep things light.

Apparently it had been the perfect thing to say. Bradley burst into a sunny smile and announced, "You're kidding! I teach sixth!"

Debbie relaxed as they launched into a discussion of school district politics. She scolded herself for thinking she needed Suz. It wasn't as if she didn't have a personality! She was smart and funny. Bradley moved on to talking about diving, the reason he'd come to Grand Cayman. Debbie mentally checked her face, making sure she wasn't wearing that vacant smile she sometimes had. She tried to concentrate on what Bradley was saying but listening wasn't any fun without the anticipation of telling Suz all about it. They loved to interpret, analyze, diagnose, evaluate, and translate every scrap of conversation and body language. Debbie realized she'd just missed half of what Bradley said and knew for sure that she was wearing her vacant smile.

A burst of laughter from the three women at the bar caught her attention. She glanced at them and realized they'd been monitoring her exchange with Bradley, just like she and Suz would have done. She felt embarrassed, but didn't hold it against them. In fact, she wished she could trade places with one of those women, be at the spectator table, sharing the jokes, predicting the next move.

Bradley ordered key lime pie which he insisted on sharing with her. Two forks, one slice. Things were moving too quickly but Suz wasn't there to suggest something to slow down the evening, like volleyball on the beach or even cards. Suz knew about pacing. Debbie usually just followed the guy's lead. She didn't understand men the way other women seemed to. She couldn't sort out what she wanted and what she didn't want, at least not quickly enough.

When she and Bradley got up from their table, the women at the bar were silent. Debbie imagined them bursting into laughter once again as the door swung shut behind her and Bradley leaving the restaurant.

Debbie didn't exactly regret the evening with Bradley. She liked him. He was a bit aggressive maybe, but in a direct, listening way. He was funny, relaxed, and in spite of his minor obsession with diving, interested in hearing about her collection of hand-painted plates, her nieces and nephews, Suz, and her other trips. He made love considerately and Debbie felt selfish and mean-spirited when her stomach turned at the curly black fur covering his pale arms, legs, chest, and back. She hated the way she was so critical of men's bodies.

She had left afterwards and returned to her own cabin, explaining to Bradley that having only arrived this afternoon she wanted to settle in. He was disappointed and suggested breakfast in the morning. She declined. She wished she knew how much longer he was scheduled to be on the island. Avoiding him for a full week in this remote place would be impossible. In the shower that night, she actually found a couple of his hairs on her body.

The next morning it was still pouring. Debbie showered again and put on her bathing suit. It was plenty warm. The rain didn't have to stop her from swimming. If she saw Bradley, she'd tell him . . . what? She needed time alone? She wasn't that kind of girl and regretted it? Suz would say, "Just tell him you can't stand hairy men." Or if Suz felt irritable, she might say, "There's always something that bothers you. Why can't you just live with it?"

Suz was right about that. When it came to men, Debbie knew she was too critical. Carl slurped when he got excited talking, which he did often, and it drove her so crazy she broke up with him. Simon wore his hair in a little ponytail which Suz thought looked fine, kind of hip, but it bugged Debbie so much that, in spite of his perfect body, she broke up with him. Wesley picked his toes. Monty permed his hair. Ian had too many pets, including an iguana and a rat. Russell was a competitive swimmer and shaved his legs and armpits. Mark taught eighth grade and Debbie had a rule against dating other teachers, which, according to Suz, had no basis in anything close to rational. Debbie particularly liked the rule now, however, because she realized it could be used for Bradley instead of hairiness. She wouldn't feel so guilty. "I don't think you like men," Suz had said once.

"I just like them too much," Debbie joked. "I can't settle for just one." She hated that Suz had said that. She liked men a lot, but none of them fit.

Debbie waded out into the rough water and once she was waist-deep, dove in. She swam hard until she reached the place where the shelf dropped off, making the water appear black rather than gray. Though she was a strong swimmer the depth made her panic. She turned and swam as fast as she could for shore.

It rained for six days. She told Bradley on the second day, when he finally tracked her down in the late afternoon, that she hadn't wanted anything romantic this trip. She needed time to herself. He was disappointed, but respected her decision. They still went to the museum together one afternoon and hand-painted plate shopping another. The rest of the time Debbie read books in her room and when that got too depressing, hunted for shells in the rain and then left them for other people to discover. The time beat on her like waves on a rock, leaving her insides bare and worn feeling. She hardly knew what to think about. She felt a tremendous sense of longing, but couldn't figure out what she wanted. On her second-to-last night on the island, she agreed to go dancing with Bradley. He wanted her to sleep with him and she did, because of that longing, but the sex only intensified it. Again, she returned to her own cabin afterwards.

The next morning, her last day on the island, Debbie awoke at dawn as the sun staggered in her window like a drunk coming home several days late. Though it was just five-thirty she put on her suit. Wading out into the sea, now flat and uniform as an Oklahoma sky, she felt tired somehow. The loneliness had hollowed her out. This morning's pink sand and robin's egg blue water, the fragile warmth of the sun, the way the sea consumed her body, felt like pain. It was all too beautiful to bear.

Debbie treated herself to a nice lunch. Being alone for so long intensified her senses. Each bite of conch steak tasted like a chewy bit of heaven. The dry, malted flavor of her beer was a perfect counter taste to the garlic butter sauce. The marinated tomatoes were tangy and fresh. The fried plantains were sweet and crispy. She ordered two slices of key lime pie, the island specialty, and ate them both. She didn't feel particularly happy, but she felt very alive.

After lunch, Debbie laid out her towel on a chair under the cabaña. Then she went in snorkeling. The fish were spectacular. Her favorite were the big ones striped pink, blue, and green, though she also loved the yolk yellow ones with black eyes. She floated for a while just above a school of electric blue fish. In her blue suit, she wondered if they thought she belonged. To test the idea she rotated her body slightly, and all the fish responded in unison, turning with her. She turned again and so did the school of fish. Then she dove underwater to see if she could swim amongst them and the fish scattered. As she resurfaced she crashed into a pair of flippers.

"Sorry," Debbie said, spitting out her snorkel mouthpiece.

"It's okay." It was one of the women who'd been at the bar in the restaurant that first night. "Finally a decent day, huh?" the woman asked.

"Yeah," Debbie said. "Unfortunately it's my last."

The woman rolled her eyes. "Ours too."

Later, as Debbie emerged from the water, she saw that the three women had settled onto lounge chairs near hers under the cabaña.

"Hope we're not crowding you," said the prettiest one, a thin blonde with a model's face, only strained looking, as if she were a little hungry and her contact lenses were uncomfortable.

The one she'd bumped into in the water held a pitcher of peach-colored drink. She was plump and had shoulder-length black hair. "Barb, honey," she said to the third, a bigger blonde with a prominent nose and an eager-looking mouth, "run get another cup. You'll have some rum punch, won't you?" she asked Debbie.

"Sure," Debbie said. "Thanks."

"I'm Roz," said the dark-haired one. "That," pointing with the pitcher, and sloshing a little, at the woman walking back to the bar, "is Barb. This is Connie, my little sister."

Roz had a great smile. It reminded Debbie of Suz's smile, cockeyed with dimples.

"*Younger* sister," the strained blonde, Connie, said.

Barb returned with the extra cup and Roz poured four rum punches. They stretched out on their towels on the chairs.

"I'm Debbie."

"We know," said Barb, and Roz fired her a dirty look. "I mean, we overheard your name the other night in the restaurant."

"It's okay," Debbie said, embarrassed.

"We couldn't help noticing that you're the only one getting any action on this beach," Barb said.

"Speak for yourself," Connie corrected.

Barb ignored Connie and added, "And he's so cute."

Debbie smelled tension, but politely answered Barb. "Yeah, he is nice-looking."

"Nice-looking, nothin'," Barb bellowed. "He's a doll."

"Here's to your continued luck." Roz plucked the paper umbrella out of the pitcher and put it in Debbie's drink.

"Why are you traveling alone?" Barb composed her face, as if she were trying to control her curiosity. Debbie could tell that she hoped for a broken engagement, confessions of nymphomania, something juicy.

Debbie tried to smile as she briefly explained about Suz getting married. She noticed Roz studying her.

"There he is," Connie said. All four women looked down the beach at a man and woman approaching, holding hands.

"Drop it, Connie," Roz said, her face tightening.

Barb's eyes lit up and she turned to Debbie and opened her mouth.

"Never mind, Barb," Roz warned.

Barb ignored her and said, "They're in number fourteen. He's a doctor. Connie's interested."

"You have such a big mouth," Roz said.

Barb's eyes shone and she kept them on Debbie, waiting for her reaction. Debbie kept quiet.

Roz smiled at her and shook her head slowly. Debbie smiled back.

Connie said, "I don't care if you want to talk about it." She reached over and touched Debbie's arm. "For god's sake, if we're drinking rum punch together, girls, we may as well get basic."

"My sister," Roz said, obliging Connie, "doesn't think marriage matters. She's been with married men before."

Debbie nodded nervously. The couple was nearly within earshot.

Roz rolled her eyes. "You know how the babies in families are. They want it, they take it."

"Don't be mean," Connie said. "I have a whole different perspective than you, and you know it. I've been married. When you've been there, done that, believe me, it looks a lot different."

"Hi Tom, Anna," Roz called out to the couple. "Finally some sunshine, huh?"

"I love it!" Anna shouted to the sky. She was very tall and wore her hair very short. Debbie wondered if she knew about Connie's designs for her husband.

"Join us?" Connie asked. Tom stood slightly behind his wife and smiled at Connie.

"Actually," Anna said, "we were just heading up to the restaurant for a bite."

"Later," Tom said, and they left.

After a long tense silence Roz said, "That was sleazy, Tom saying 'Later.' I can't believe you'd do that to another woman."

"You have to get over thinking marriage is holy," Connie cut in.

Barb leaned toward Debbie and offered, "Anna is going to see a friend in town tonight. Tom invited Connie over for drinks in his cabin."

"It's my last day of vacation and it has been a dry one," Connie said defensively.

"Thanks," Roz said. "Loved your company, too."

"Oh, you know what I mean."

"Not really." Roz took a deep breath and looked out at the sea. The water was all diamonds now. She turned to Debbie. "I guess I've gotten to the point where I think there's a hell of a lot more to life than men."

Debbie took a big gulp of rum punch. She felt excited. More had happened in this half-hour under the cabaña than had happened all week. With women there was always suspense about something. With men she too often felt as if she were headed for some kind of specific conclusion. Here, under the cabaña, were four lives bursting with possibility.

"So how'd your friend—Suz?—meet the guy she married?" Barb asked.

"On a hiking trip in the Southwest. Gregory was one of the guides." She didn't mention how Gregory had been interested in her first. Debbie thought he was too much like a large dog—every muscle always twitching, eager to the point of salivating.

Roz looked thoughtful. "We should do that," she said to Barb. "An *activity* vacation."

"Do you think it's a good marriage?" Barb asked.

"You think any marriage is a good marriage."

"Give us a break, Connie. You are so jaded."

"I just want some action, I don't care about marriage. Marriage is a lie."

Roz sighed. She reached over and patted her sister's hand. "Let's get another pitcher."

Everyone threw in a couple of dollars and Connie went to get the rum punch. Debbie felt pretty tipsy already.

"I'm ready for a splash. Wanna come?" Roz addressed Debbie.

"Sure." The two women waded out into the sea together, then Roz dove in and swam fifty yards. Debbie followed her. Roz flipped over on her back and floated. "It's heaven!" she called out. "Let's swim to the reef."

The reef was another hundred yards, well beyond the line dividing the shallow and deep water, but as Debbie passed over into the deep water she felt only a little frightened. She liked Roz's spunk.

The waves splashing against the reef were gentle today and Roz climbed right out of the water onto the coral.

"We'll shred our feet!" Debbie yelled, climbing after her. Roz reached down and pulled Debbie up by the hand. A thin stream of blood ran down from her knee where she'd banged it on the coral, but she didn't feel any pain. She felt wonderful in fact, full of salt water, hard breathing and thick, sweet sunshine. The two women each put an arm around the other's shoulder. With their free hands, they waved at the dots under the tiny cabaña back on the beach.

"Don't you wish the week were just beginning?" Debbie asked.

Roz looked at her quickly and dropped her arm. "Yes," she

said. "You should have joined us earlier." Then she dove off the reef.

Debbie had meant the sunshine, but felt thrilled that Roz meant her company.

A few minutes later they dragged out of the water, dripping wet and laughing hysterically. Connie poured them fresh rum punches. "Drink up, girls."

"Look who's coming," Roz said, toweling her hair. Debbie looked down the beach and there was Bradley approaching in khaki shorts and no shirt.

"Handsome!" Barb said and Debbie turned to see if she was joking. Who could like all that hair?

Bradley said, "Hi," and sat on the edge of Debbie's lounge chair. She moved her legs so that he wasn't pushed against them. He gazed at her happily.

"Have a good dive?" she asked. It must have been later than Debbie thought if he was already back from his afternoon dive.

"Super," he beamed, obviously impatient to tell her more.

"Where'd you dive?" Barb chirped. Apparently she used a different voice, in a higher register, with men. She looked very attentive as he answered.

Connie suddenly sat up in her chair. Debbie saw Tom, alone, walking back to his and Anna's cabin. He waved.

Roz smirked at her sister. "I advise you one last time, don't do it," she said.

"Don't do what?" Bradley asked cheerfully.

Connie stood and stretched. "Time," she said, "for me to have a shower and freshen up for the evening."

Debbie got a feeling of impending desertion as Connie walked away. The afternoon seemed to have just begun. She wished the four of them—her, Roz, Barb, and Connie—could chat under the cabaña all evening.

Bradley wouldn't stop smiling at her. Barb kept smiling at Bradley. When Bradley went to get a cup so he could have some rum punch, Debbie whispered to Barb, "Go for it. I'm serious. I'm not even remotely interested. You'd be doing me a favor."

Barb looked at her like she was crazy and said, "Are you sure?"

"Positive."

"Well, obviously he adores *you*, anyway."

"Secretly," Roz said sadly, her gaze following her sister up the beach, "Connie always hopes these guys will leave their wives for her."

This news disappointed Debbie. She didn't think she liked Connie, but she liked her hard edge.

Roz continued, "Especially the doctor-types."

"What do *you* want in a man?" Debbie suddenly asked Roz.

"Honesty, sense of humor, stability." She batted out the qualities quickly, as if she'd rehearsed them.

But what *else*? a voice inside Debbie insisted. Was she the only one who asked that question?

"Passion," Barb sighed.

Debbie and Roz both turned and stared.

Yeah, Debbie thought, a gut-wrenching feeling, like when she and Suz laughed so hard she got stomach cramps and still they didn't stop. Or like that time when she and Suz couldn't find a room in Venice, so instead they walked along the canals all night talking about absolutely every last dream they'd ever had, blissful in spite of exhaustion and the foul smell of the water. The feeling that what's between you and this person is all you need to survive.

Bradley returned with his cup and Debbie said, "Roz," nodding her head down the beach. Roz got up and they walked a bit. "Just thought I'd give them some time alone," Debbie said.

"You're too much," Roz smiled and took her arm.

Later, Debbie thought, after Bradley and Barb left, she and Roz could get their own pitcher of rum punch. They could spend the evening debating what was going on in cabin fourteen, Tom's, and cabin five, Bradley's. They could talk about a lot of other things too. In fact, maybe they wouldn't talk about Bradley or Tom at all. There were a million other things she'd like to know about Roz.

Roz said, "I wasn't about to mention it to that viper pit, meaning around Barb and Connie, but I've got a date tonight myself."

Debbie's insides plummeted. "Wow," she forced. "You do?"

"Yeah, a scuba diver." Roz elbowed her gently. "What else is there around here? He's nice-looking though, about ten years older than me."

"When's your date?"

"About an hour and a half. I'd better get going."

Debbie made herself smile. "Have fun!" She waded ankle-deep into the Caribbean, then turned around and watched Roz climb the stairs to the cabins. Debbie wished she'd asked Roz what it felt like for her when she touched a man.

She looked back at the cabaña. She hoped to see Bradley earnestly telling Barb the details of his dive, but he was looking down the beach at her. He waved when he saw her looking. In a minute, he would excuse himself, leave Barb, and come to her.

Debbie slipped into the sea and swam fast and hard toward to reef. When she reached it she climbed out again as she had done with Roz. First she looked back at Cayman Kai Resort. A dark figure was walking toward the place she'd entered the water. Another figure stirred under the cabaña, probably gathering her things to return to her cabin. Debbie turned and walked across the reef, wincing as her feet landed on the sharp coral. She stood facing the open sea, the profoundly blue water beyond the enclosure of the reef. Jamaica lay to the east, the next island over.

Suddenly she leapt into the deep water separating the islands, excited rather than afraid of the depth. As she flipped over on her back to float, a clean thought came to her: She didn't have to do anything she didn't want to do. Not one single thing. From this moment on. These thoughts cleared out space for a flood of crystalline feeling. Bright fishes, conch shells, palm fronds, purple coral fans, the liquid bliss of the sea itself, these were her feelings, and though they were just a beginning, they were finally pure.

SWEAT

SHARON KISSES the three state championship trophies as she always does before leaving her locker room office. She doesn't have to walk through the gymnasium to get to her car, but she always does that too. This evening particularly she needs to breathe in its musky smell of sweat-soaked wood and listen to her sneakers squeak across the varnished floor. When the lights are up and she's running a practice, she thinks only of how well her players execute their skills. But in the evenings, alone in the dark gymnasium, she thinks of past seasons. She's had a fine career, so fine she's been offered a college position.

Sharon stops in the middle of the gymnasium floor, not wanting to go home. "You're forty-three already," Ann, her lover of fifteen years, had shouted this morning. "Shit or get off the pot." Ann wants her to take the college job. It'd be more money.

Money and sex, it's all they ever fight about. Not enough of either for Ann. An accountant, she'd recently pushed her salary into six figures. They bought a luxury house which Sharon can't afford. Ann said don't sweat it, she'd cover it, but now, a year later, Ann would like more help with the mortgage. Sharon misses their former home, small and snug.

Sharon eyes the basket then trots up the key, gently tossing her briefcase toward the hoop. As she catches it, someone says, "Ms. Barnaby?"

Sharon whirls around. Her star point guard sits on the bottom bleacher with a basketball at her hip, still in practice shorts and jersey. Monica is short and chunky with long, curly, light brown hair. Her eyes are the color of cocoa.

"What are you doing here, Monica? It's five o'clock. Didn't you shower?"

"I've been practicing my free throw."

She's lying. From her office in the locker room Sharon can hear every ball bounce. Monica is trying to win her favor. Sharon has been asking her to work on her free throw all season. She's an expert at drawing fouls but she doesn't follow through at the goal. She bets Monica has been napping on the bleachers. She's noticed before that the girl avoids home.

"Help me with my free throw?" she asks.

"You have to leave now. Tomorrow in practice I will."

"Just ten minutes. Please?"

"Mr. Sorenson stays every evening until six o'clock," Sharon tells her and immediately regrets it. Why had she mentioned the principal? What did he have to do with anything? She'd spoken as if she were Monica's peer and Mr. Sorenson the authority, limiting what they both want. Sharon doesn't want to stay here and work on Monica's free throw. She doesn't want to go home and face Ann either. Trying to explain herself, she adds, "All students are supposed to be out of the building by five."

The custodian shoves open the gymnasium door. He doesn't notice the woman and girl standing in the dark under a basketball hoop. He checks something in a circuit panel and then leaves again. Sharon notices she has held her breath. She is grateful that

Monica remained silent, then wonders why she cares. Sharon often feels that she is hiding, even when she isn't.

Monica stretches and repeats her request. "Ten minutes, Ms. Barnaby. Then I'll leave."

The custodian comes in again. This time he flips on the lights. "You still here, Coach?" he calls out cheerfully.

"Yeah," Sharon says quickly. She looks at her watch. Five fifteen. "We were doing a little free throw practice."

Monica's face is impassive. Sharon is mortified that she lied in front of the girl. And why?

"Then you'll need the lights," the custodian suggests.

"No," Sharon says firmly. "Thank you. We're done."

"Good night then, Coach." The custodian salutes and leaves.

Monica moves to the foul line at the top of the key. She stands with her fingers spread around the ball. Sharon puts down her briefcase and kicks it gently away from the key. It slides easily on the polished floor.

Instead of shooting a free throw Monica motions as if she is going to drive to the basket.

The challenge stirs Sharon. She steps in front of Monica and says, "Just try it."

Monica fakes left, goes right. As she leaps for the shot, Sharon pops the ball out of her hands without touching her. "Try again," Sharon says, retrieving the ball and passing it forcefully to Monica. The girl's eyes shine with amazement. Sharon guesses Monica thought she could get by her old coach.

This time Monica drives straight forward, then drops back for a quick turn-around jump shot. Sharon stuffs that one.

"Wow, Ms. Barnaby."

Sharon feels a rich power in her belly. She never plays with the girls. It's a rule. She has nothing to prove, and yet this evening the competition feels like a drug. Monica is the best point guard she's ever had. After ten minutes of play she hasn't scored once, not once, on Sharon.

Not bad for a forty-three-year-old has-been, she says in her mind to Ann, whom she knows could care less about how well Sharon plays defense. Sharon wishes she hadn't thought of Ann. She'd tried to call her all day but never got past the secretary. Which means Ann told her secretary to tell Sharon she was unavailable. Increasingly, Ann runs all aspects of her life like a set of books, keeping track of every single interaction.

With a double fake, Monica finally gets past Sharon and stops short for a bank shot. She misses and Sharon beats her to the board. Sharon tosses the ball to Monica.

"You go," Monica says, firing the ball back and breaking a silence that has carried them through several plays. She adds, "I need to practice my D."

Sharon takes the ball to the top of the key. Monica plays her close, resting one hand lightly on Sharon's hip. The girl's curls are dark with sweat and plastered around her ears and neck. She's breathing harder than Sharon.

"0-0," Sharon says, and Monica's eyes widen with surprise that Sharon is keeping track of the score. Monica steels herself, the competition cinching a tension between them. Sharon drives left, hooks right, and gets her own board, popping in a lay-up. She'd left Monica under the left side of the basket, awed.

"1-0." This time Monica plays even tighter defense, insisting with her whole body that her coach will not get by her. She stays at Sharon's side all the way to the hoop, fouling with her full-body press as Sharon goes up for the point. Sharon doesn't call the foul.

"2-0." On the next play, Sharon misses the shot and Monica gets the rebound. The play gets rougher. Monica drives directly into Sharon, then rolls off her as if a pick had been set, and takes the ball to the hoop. She makes the shot.

Sharon swats her behind, congratulating her even though she's angry she gave away a point. That would be the last one. The desire to win, by the biggest possible margin, thickens in her blood.

At the top of the key, Monica dribbles once and Sharon steals the ball. They trade places and Monica sets herself up for defense. She presses so close that Sharon can feel the sweat from Monica's thigh seep into her own warm-ups. Sharon pauses a minute, waiting for her to back off, but she doesn't. They have silently agreed to a no-fouls rule, but playing this close is bad defense. Sharon rolls past her, feeling Monica's hands brush her behind, and lays in a simple goal.

Soon, exultant, Sharon says, "10-2, I win."

"Let's play full-court," Monica dares.

The girl won't quit. She figures she can win on endurance alone.

They start at mid-court. Sharon lets Monica go first. Monica is fast and the scoring is even as they race up and down the length of the court. The fouls get much rougher. Monica grabs Sharon's shooting arm while she goes up for a lay-up. Sharon seizes the waistband of Monica's shorts when she drives past her. They don't lose contact even while dribbling down court to the opposite goal. When Sharon goes up for game point, Monica wraps both arms around her middle and pulls her away from the basket.

"Hey!" Sharon cries the first protest as the ball falls through the hoop anyway. She drops back down to her feet, still in the circle of Monica's arms, as if she were a ball and Monica the hoop.

"You win," Monica says.

Sharon feels as if she's been tuned. Every atom in her body is radiating in sync. "Yep, I win," she says.

Monica's cocoa eyes are big and needy. Sharon can see that the game has affected her differently. It hasn't satisfied, it has whetted. Losing can be like that. Though Monica drops her arms, they stand so close that Sharon feels the girl's breasts heave with exhausted panting. Monica, a foot shorter than Sharon, drops her forehead onto her coach's chest for a moment, then looks up. Sharon leans down and lightly kisses her lips. Monica's eyes change. Fear mixes in with the neediness. Even so, she places her hands around Sharon's neck and returns the kiss, hard, hungrily. Then she wrenches free, as if Sharon had been holding her there.

Monica backs away from her coach. Her mouth begins to twist into an ugly shape. "Mr. Sorenson," she whispers.

A deep, enormous silence opens up in Sharon's chest. She says, "Don't, Monica. Don't do it."

"Mr. Sorenson," Monica screams. "Mr. Sorenson!"

Sharon watches the girl turn and sprint toward the gymnasium door. The door swings shut behind Monica with a loud clang. Sharon stands sweating, alone in the dark gymnasium.

THE NIGHT DANNY WAS RAPED

THE NIGHT Danny was raped, his rapist came to my lover's room.

I am eighteen years old, naked, and crammed in a closet. The odor of sweaty sneakers assaults my nose. Wool pants that smell like mildew hang in my face. A loose hanger, tangled in with the shoes on the floor, jabs dangerously close to my genitals. I think how much Danny will enjoy hearing about this scenario. Suppressing a giggle, I shift and a shoe slides off another and thuds to the floor. I freeze. The voices in the room outside the closet stop. Then I hear Angela's nervous laugh. She is the one who pushed me in here just moments ago when someone knocked on her dorm room door. She is afraid not to answer her door, believing that the person on the outside will know that she is inside having sex. With another girl. She is afraid that even if I dress and greet the visitor with her, he will smell the sex in the room and know.

Angela is afraid. Her charm is her defense. She cultivates other people's affections like we are all plants on her farm. Her friends flock to her dorm room any time of day and night and Angela is compelled to attend to each of them. If she does not they will know. Now that I have knocked over a shoe, made noise, she will keep her visitor, Bob, the man who raped Danny, even longer, to prove she is hiding nothing.

Bob is a yellow-blond white man, trying to convince Angela, my black girlfriend, to go to a movie with him. But really, he is trying to convince her to go to bed with him. "Come on, Ange, why not? What else you gonna do tonight?" I can picture his half-smile, the expression on his face that shows he thinks he's getting something.

I am eighteen years old, a naked white girl, crammed in a closet on a snowy evening in New England. I am listening to my lover play along with this man coming on to her—or is she playing?—because she does not want anyone to think she is a lesbian.

I do not yet know that Bob raped Danny earlier this evening. I do know that this intruder interrupted Angela's and my love-making. This man asked for my lover's attention and got it on demand.

The night Danny was raped, his rapist came to my lover's room while I sat in the closet, naked, and thought of my brothers, the first men in my life.

I am two years old. My family is vacationing in California and I toddle into the deep end of the motel swimming pool and begin to drown. Bubbles float to the surface as my fat little body rapidly sinks. Greg, my ten-year-old brother, dives into the pool. Despite the weight of his water-logged Converse sneakers and blue jeans with the six-inch cuffs, he grabs me around the tummy, kicks to the surface, and swims to the pool's edge. I learn at age two that for the rest of my life my brother will protect me.

I am ten years old. I stand with the bat cocked expertly over my right shoulder, feet spread, and my eye on the ball in Charlie's fist.

Charlie, my other brother, is twelve years old and the strongest pitcher in his league.

"Whatever you do," he tells me, "do not take your eye off the ball. Do not swing. Do not move. Not an inch."

Charlie winds up and pitches the hardball, overhand, at me with as much force as he can. It thuds into my left hip and the pain soars down my leg and up my side. I do not take my eye off the ball. I do not swing.

"You moved. Again."

Charlie pitches several more hardballs at my body until my left side throbs from the assaults. Finally satisfied, he says, "You won't be afraid of the ball anymore." And I am proud.

My brothers are the men in my life. I love them with all my heart. I date only their friends in high school. I measure all men against my brothers. I am not prepared to know Danny.

The night Danny was raped, his rapist came to my lover's room while I sat in the closet, naked, and thought of my brothers, the first men in my life, who caught me in an early act of lesbian separatism.

I am twelve years old, naked, and lying in the attic with my best friend Nicole. Below me in the family room the men in my life watch the Superbowl. I hear the pumped up voices from the tube: "He's *down* on the ten yard line" and "It's a long shot to the wide receiver." I hear the joy in my brothers' laughter as they shout at good and bad plays and I recognize that their joy stems from not just the game, but from the maleness of the game. I am not a part of the football game and I do not care. I choose to ignore the men in my family, I choose to ignore football. They do not know I am choosing something other than them, but I know it. Up in the attic, above the family room, above the Superbowl,

I search Nicole's child's body and find a strength in her that kicks at my gut, more powerful than the arms of my brother when I am drowning, more explosively sensational to my body than any hardball. I sense the promise of everything I am looking for right there under my hands and in my mouth.

The attic has no floor, just long rafters across which we put a piece of plywood. On either side of the plywood are pockets of dust and below that the ceiling tiles of the family room. I like the feel of the cool plywood against my back as Nicole touches me. Later, still naked, something prods me to explore deeper in the attic and I crawl along one of those rafters with Nicole right behind me. My knee misses the rafter and plunges into the dust. I lose my balance altogether and fall off the rafter. I crash through the family room ceiling, up to my waist. I am gripping the rafter with my hands and Nicole holds me by the armpits. Below, the men in my family view my bare bum and dangling legs. I believe they also view all the potency that I have discovered in Nicole's body, my secret. There is silence except for the television. No one speaks of the naked little girl dangling above them. Nicole hauls me back up in the attic and my indiscretion is never mentioned, though the ceiling is quickly repaired.

For ten years, I loathe this memory.

The night Danny was raped, his rapist came to my lover's room while I sat in the closet, naked, and thought of my brothers, the first men in my life, who caught me in an early act of lesbian separatism, until Angela left with the rapist.

My muscles ache from my cramped position in Angela's closet as I hear her leave with Bob, the man who earlier in the evening raped Danny, though I do not know this yet. I wonder what she expects of me: to stay in the closet until she returns, just in case?

"I called the dean and told him," Danny tells me.

I feel myself plummet through the family room ceiling again, hang there naked. How could Danny expose himself like that? I am amazed that Danny would ask for help so readily and almost angry at what I perceive as his privilege to do so.

I tell Danny that I hope Bob is expelled, because I think that is what Danny wants, and I leave.

The night Danny was raped, his rapist came to my lover's room while I sat in the closet, naked, and thought of my brothers, the first men in my life, who caught me in an early act of lesbian separatism, until Angela left with the rapist, and then I went to Danny's room, where he and I tried to make love, after which I walked back to my own room wondering if Angela was fucking Danny's rapist.

It is cold, clear, and I wear sneakers in the wet snow. I let my feet get very wet and very cold until they ache. The bare elm trees loom overhead. I feel as if Bob is lurking in the dark. I feel hunted by him, though it is not my body I am afraid for, but somehow, my soul.

When I reach my room, I call Danny. I tell him, "Angela went off with Bob before I came over to your room."

Danny gasps dramatically, as if this is any old gossip, and I am relieved. We settle into the confines of our friendship as we'd known it before tonight. I tell him about the closet and he dies laughing. We talk on the phone for two and a half hours. It is just like old times. When I finally hang up, the phone rings right away and it is Angela. She's been trying to call all night. Will I come over? I come. She says she did not fuck Bob. I do not and I do believe her.

I guess that Danny would roll his eyes if I told him what Angela

I kick open the door and stand to stretch my legs.

The door to Angela's dorm room cracks open. It is too late to cover my nakedness. It is only Angela who winks at me and whispers, "Sorry, sweetheart. What could I tell him? I'll see you later."

"Fuck you," I mutter. She pours into the room and carefully shuts the door behind her, then rushes over to kiss me. I am easily pacified. I am devoted to this woman's kisses. I will try to understand.

And I do. Somewhat. Angela is one of a tiny handful of black students on this small, very white liberal arts campus. For her coming out means alienating her peers, her small community of support. She cannot afford to do that and I have to concur that on a campus this small, you are out unless you prove that you are actively in, which is what Angela is trying to do.

I let her go with Bob and steel myself against the pain. Another hardball. I am well-trained. I do not avert my eyes. I do not swing. I do not move.

I am eighteen years old and scared to death, though I will not admit this because I can take any hardball that comes my way. I am a white girl from Oregon on a very white, small New England campus and I am drowning because I do not know how to drink cocktails and I do not own an evening gown. I do not yet consider myself an adult, though my classmates have been thinking of themselves that way for five years. I am a lesbian separatist by default, though I do not call myself this and never will. I understand loyalty, men to men and women to women, because that was how I was raised. I am shattered that my lover has walked out for the night with a man who I do not know at the time is Danny's rapist. But he is. And he asked for my lover's attention and got it. On demand.

• • •

The night Danny was raped, his rapist came to my lover's room while I sat in the closet, naked, and thought of my brothers, the first men in my life, who caught me in an early act of lesbian separatism, until Angela left with the rapist, and then I went to Danny's room, where he and I tried to make love.

The night is cold and clear. There is a foot of snow on the ground and my breath makes dense clouds in the air. I arrive at Danny's dorm.

Danny seems delighted to see me. He is shriekier than usual, wired, and I wonder if I want to stay. He launches into a story about a gay professor whom he saw in a gay bar in Boston and how the teacher wouldn't speak to him and we die laughing at how this professor dates a female literature professor on campus to protect himself. I don't feel like telling Danny about the closet anymore. And I don't want to think about Bob and Angela. So I suggest that Danny and I do what we'd talked about doing.

He balks, "You mean . . . ?"

"We don't have to," I say. It's not like I'm hot for him or anything.

"Let's!" Danny is suddenly ready. When we had once talked about sleeping together, we thought of it as a last hurrah, or maybe a final test, just to make sure we didn't really want heterosexuality after all. Later, I wonder why he agrees to this tonight. Perhaps he is hungry to be held. Perhaps I am too, though I do not admit this to myself.

Danny is a thin, nervous gay Jewish boy from New York. His fear of life is palpable, it's in the very paleness of his skin, the suddenness of his donkey-like laugh. Danny is my first gay male friend and I love him for his love of gossip, for his easy vulnerability. I feel like a rock next to his ghost. I trust Danny because he seems powerless.

Danny and I touch one another and laugh at the oddness of the

other's body. I run my fingers through the thick hair on his thin chest. I touch his bony hips, his floppy penis. His kisses are too sloppy. Wet with intent rather than passion.

By the way he touches my breasts I know he is slightly repulsed. My flesh feels like modeling clay under his hands.

I finally slap his hairy butt, he screeches, and we give up. After all, we tried.

Then, lying naked on his narrow dorm bed, he tells me about Bob.

Just a few hours earlier, the big blond boy came to his room on the pretext of borrowing some physics notes and shoved Danny onto his own bed. He stripped off Danny's corduroy pants and raped him. Danny tells me every detail and he is shaking.

I listen. But. This is not easy vulnerability. This is raw exposure. I feel as if Danny is an antique goblet shattering in my hands. I am powerless, even more powerless than Danny because I am holding the shards that could shred me to ribbons.

I am eighteen years old. I wonder. Who is this boy named Danny? He is not my brother.

Danny is unusually calm. He sits up and puts on his glasses. He walks hunched over, so I won't see his genitals, to get his pants and pulls them on. I grasp for my own clothes, suddenly desperate to cover my nakedness.

We are not talking now. My mind is careening. Angela just left with Danny's rapist, though I do not tell Danny this, and I do not know where they went. I feel trapped with Danny as if we were both caught in a shameful act. I do not tell Danny that I spent a lot of time shut in my lover's closet earlier this evening. It doesn't seem funny now. I do not tell him that his rapist is with my lover. My heart is reeling. Away from Danny.

I demand to know. "What are you going to *do*?" I understand action.

claims. But Danny and I do not speak of this evening ever again. In fact, we speak little in the spring that follows. We say we are busy. The truth is that in spite of our two and a half hour phone talk that was just like old times, it really isn't like old times anymore. We know too much and we know too little. About each other. Danny graduates in May and I put him out of my mind.

Years later I learn that he is a very successful businessman in New York. This information surprises me because I do not see Danny as someone that powerful. And it threatens me because—although I can take it—I no longer trust people who wield hardballs. And I remember his easy access to the dean. I remember that Bob was expelled the following day.

Even so, one warm summer evening in Oregon I call directory assistance in New York and find his number. I dial eagerly. The voice on the machine is definitely Danny's. I leave a message, long and excited, and hang up. Danny never calls me back.

I tell myself, "He's a big shot now. Wouldn't you know he'd turn his back on his lesbian sister, merely a struggling writer."

But an ugly feeling burrows into my gut like an escaping rodent. I know that I had not allowed Danny to be anyone but my brother, and he certainly wasn't that, so to me Danny was never really anyone. At eighteen I had never known a boy who could need something from a girl. I had never known a man who would expose himself to the public, to a dean. I had never known a man who didn't associate the body with either shame or power. I was eighteen years old and I loved my brothers who protected me and taught me to be tough. They were my world of men. I realize now that there was a way that Danny's rapist, the man who wooed my lover, got more of my attention, and maybe even respect, than Danny. He got it on demand.

Today I am thirty-five years old. I miss Danny. I especially miss all the parts of him that I couldn't see and never knew. I pick up the phone and call New York's directory assistance again. The operator says there are now five people by that name living in Manhattan. She refuses to give me five numbers. I call directory assistance eleven times until I get an operator who agrees to give me all five numbers. Tonight I will begin dialing, looking for Danny.

THE RESCUE

THE NATIONAL ENDOWMENT for the Arts refused to fund my collection of lesbian erotica, forcing me to take a job in the financial district, where I copied, filed, and made coffee for Meredith, an advertising exec. Meredith liked me. A lot. On the nights when her live-in boyfriend, Douglas, was busy, she coerced me into going out for drinks. I'd thrill her with lies about my sex life and she'd whine about Douglas.

Have a little compassion for me when I admit that I developed a crush on the woman. I was trapped on the tenth floor of an urban nightmare, a glass and metal building, surrounded by a secretarial pool wearing glasses with crooked temples and rhinestone implants. The corporate bosses, men and women, had such phony faces I felt I could take hold of the edges and rip them off. That I had the creativity to conceive of and then nurture a crush in that environment says a lot about my vision.

Meredith wore gender bender girl suits on her butch body. Picture a woman who looked like a man trying to look like a woman dressed like a man. I took her long, confidential diatribes against her boyfriend as early signs of coming out, and entertained myself by imagining her in Levi's, a white T-shirt and a black leather jacket.

One evening around six o'clock, she and I sat drinking martinis at a Civic Center fern bar. My crush was peaking, but I wasn't so far gone that I didn't feel shame. A fern bar with a woman in a suit and sneakers—how low could I sink? Thank you, Jesse Helms, this garden-variety lesbian needed that grant. At least there wasn't any chance of someone I cared about seeing me there with her.

To make matters worse, Meredith was in an appreciating-her-boyfriend mood. I spaced out while she blathered, "He's so sensitive. Can you believe he cooks dinner every Wednesday night *and* does the dishes.... He actually cries more than me at movies...."

Sicko straight girl, I thought. I tried to steer the conversation back to what a jerk Douglas was. I commented on how *hard* she worked and how *much* she deserved in the way of attention, loving. I urged her to be frank with me, to feel safe with the truth.

She turned the corner then, admitting that it would be nice if Douglas cleaned the bathroom sometimes, especially since he worked only part-time. I nodded meaningfully, staring at her with rapt attention. "Go on," I murmured.

Just then a big, mean-looking lesbian entered my peripheral vision. If Roberta Achtenberg frightened Jesse Helms, this dyke would give him a heart attack. Standing with her hands on her hips, about six feet tall and three feet wide, she perused the fern bar as if searching for the best place to set up a tent.

Then I noticed she wasn't alone. A couple dozen multiply-pierced, hairy-legged queers flooded the bar. After stomping around like barn animals for a minute or two, they coupled up and started kissing.

Gratitude exploded inside me. My people had come to rescue me. I wanted to shout, I'm here! I'm right over here!

I looked at Meredith, who had plastered a good liberal smile on her face. "This is wonderful," she muttered through tight jaws. Her legs looked more gripped than crossed.

Since Meredith was so supportive, I decided to include her. I leaned over and kissed her on the mouth. For a brief moment, her lips responded as if they had a will of their own. Then she yanked back. I hoped she hadn't given herself whiplash. She smiled hard to camouflage her terror.

Poor thing. My crush crumbled into pity.

Someone tapped me on the shoulder. It was the original six-foot Amazon. She planted a wet one on my mouth and I threw my arms around her neck so hard she grunted. By the time I opened my eyes again, Meredith was gone.

TEAMWORK

THE FIRST THING any of us noticed about Thalia Peterson was her legs. And I mean *legs*. The girl could play some serious ball too.

We all knew when she joined the team that there'd be changes. Not that we were blatant about anything, but when you work out together three to four hours a day, you get to reading each other intimately. You learn a lot about your teammates. We all knew who liked girls, who did it with boys, who hated white girls and who thought black people were dumb. We had all those kinds of people on the team, but on a good ball team you learn to respect differences and keep your eye on the ball. You become so tightly woven into each other's lives by so much sweat, by so many wins and losses, fights and tears, and mid-game highs, that you can have all your homophobia, heterophobia, racism and what have you, and still not be able to separate yourself from your teammates. On the court anyway.

Thalia Peterson was a southern white girl, big legged, with white teeth and a thick ponytail of smooth blond hair. Her eyes were both narrow-set and deep-set at the same time and had long dark lashes. She seemed farther back there than most people. I wondered if we'd ever be able to read her like we read one another. She wore make-up, too. Not that we weren't used to that. Both Kathy Jones and Amanda Severson wore make-up and of course that was their business, but Thalia's make-up was straight out of *Glamour* magazine, almost a lifestyle. She had the kind of looks boys made a point of turning and looking at, because if they didn't their manhood would be questioned. I knew she was pretty, but her looks weren't the kind I fell for. Just couldn't stomach those eyes.

Thalia Peterson was a junior like me. She'd been at the university for two years but hadn't come out for the team. End of her freshman year she pledged Phi Beta Pi, the snottiest sorority on campus, and got herself established there before revealing her jock talents. That was her business, of course, though some say she waited two years just so she could blow everyone away when she did come out for the team.

At first we kind of liked her sorority connections because suddenly our home game crowds swelled full of her Phi Beta Pi sisters and their fraternity boyfriends. The fact was, people loved to watch Thalia Peterson play ball, and I couldn't blame them. She was a big girl, strong and tall, and damn near the most aggressive ball player I've ever seen. Get up under that basket for a rebound and *boom!* she'd block you out by throwing her powerful behind into you, more often than not sending you flying across the floor. She never got fouls called on her because the refs couldn't believe someone that feminine and pretty had any *umph*. You could see a quick puzzled look cross the ref's face before he decided that Thalia's opponent must have just fallen down. *She* couldn't have pushed that girl onto the floor. Truth was, in addition to a well-aimed elbow, Thalia Peterson was very skilled in getting her body in the right place at the right time.

There was something else about Thalia Peterson. She didn't just like winning. She expected to win, even *lived* to win. In everything.

Most women on the team didn't enjoy her as much as the fans in the audience did. They didn't think it fair for Thalia to come out for the team her junior year when the rest of us had struggled up from junior varsity since freshman year. I didn't see that it mattered. But then, she didn't bump my position. I didn't have much of a position. I came off the bench as a guard when the game was clearly won or clearly lost. That was okay with me. Games scared me shitless. I played for the practices, the uniforms, the feeling of being on a team.

Some people cared a great deal about Thalia Peterson coming out her junior year. Kathy Jones for one. And Carson McDuffy for another. Kathy Jones, I already told you, wore make-up, was real skinny and gangly, and played center mostly. She was a fantastic shooter and great on boards, but inconsistent and definitely a bad ball handler. Carson McDuffy was hot. She could do everything—dribble, pass, shoot, and sometimes even rebound, though she was only five-foot-four. Her problem was that she played forward, insisted on it, in spite of her height. Her other problem was that she was hotheaded.

Carson was a very serious-minded ball player, hilarious off the court, singular in her likes and dislikes (luckily, I was one of her likes) and a lesbian. She had a medium-sized angular body, short scruffy brown hair and pale white skin. Carson had her goals set on making the Eastern Division All-Star team.

In the fall, on the first day of tryouts for the university team, Carson's confidence glowed. She made passes behind her back, crashed through a crowded key for lay-ups, and played as if the fast break was the only offensive option.

"Okay," I told her. "So you've been working out all summer.

Easy on the rest of us okay?"

She fired me one of her try-and-stop-me grins and pressed harder. The truth was she'd never looked better. I always took her with a grain of salt, she was so crazy, but her enthusiasm spurred the team on. I hoped almost as much as she did that she'd make the Eastern Division All-Star team this year.

Carson noticed Thalia Peterson during tryouts all right, and she planned on putting her in her place immediately. When Coach Montgomery shouted, "Pair up for one-on-one," Carson made her move. I saw her cock her finger, thumb up, at Thalia. "You," was all she said. Then she strode toward Thalia as if she was coming on to her. "Oh, god," I said under my breath. That woman always reminded me of lit dynamite that never quite explodes.

By instinct, the rest of us backed off the court to watch. Carson shot a bullet pass at Thalia's middle. "You go first," she said. Thalia caught the pass as gracefully as if it had been lobbed. Even before Montgomery blew the whistle Carson's hands were working Thalia, cutting the air in front of her face like blades. Thalia maintained a regal stance, casual and uninterested. The whistle blew. Thalia faked a jump shot, then moved left. Carson stayed on her, grinning and chattering like a monkey. "Go ahead, go ahead," she threatened. "Try and get around me. Try."

Thalia tried, her blond ponytail swinging back and forth on her back. When she couldn't get past Carson she stopped, figuring she could easily put up a jump shot over Carson's head. Shouting a loud war cry, Carson stuffed the attempted shot. She wiped her hands on her shorts, chased down the ball and stood at the top of the key waiting for Montgomery's whistle. That's when I first noticed how much Thalia liked to win. She was *mad*. She wore her anger like a queen, chin up and eyes smoldering like rubies. Even so, Carson drove by her three times in a row. After each goal she hooted her triumph in hyena-like howls as she trotted back up to the top of the key.

The fourth time she missed the lay-up and Thalia rebounded. It was her game after that. She'd miscalculated Carson's talents, but now that she knew them, she could meet them. Thalia faked left, drove right, stopped short, and popped a jump shot. Next she sunk a rimless goal from the top of the key, right over Carson's hands. To prove she could drive, Thalia pushed to the left, lost Carson as she cut under the basket, and hooked the ball in. At that point Coach sent Carson to the locker room for cursing out loud and Thalia toweled the back of her neck, easy and casual.

After that day we knew Carson hated Thalia, and some of us wondered if she'd quit the team if Thalia got her starting position. The other starters were Kathy Jones at center, Susan Thurmond and Jackie Sanchez (who I was beginning to fall deeply in something with) as guards, and Stella Stellason at forward. Everyone knew that Stella was sleeping with our coach, Hilary Montgomery, and nobody saw any need to do much more than raise an eyebrow. It would be one thing if Stella were no good and Montgomery were playing her all the time, something like that, but Stella was key to our team—tall, smooth, consistent, just what hotheaded Carson needed out there to shine. No way did Thalia threaten Stella's position.

Well, sure enough, the season started and Thalia wound up bumping Carson mostly. No one blamed Montgomery, except Carson. Carson had been a star all right, but she was too short and needed too much setting up. Thalia could set herself up. Besides, without Carson out there turning cartwheels to the basket, Stella was freer to show off her stuff, and she did. With Thalia on the team we stood a chance of going to the playoffs. What made me mad though was the tiny glint of triumph way back in those cryptic eyes of Thalia's. That wasn't necessary and I just knew it made Carson's blood boil.

Teams always have a lot of tension on them. Sometimes the tension is the main thing holding them together, but Thalia's presence brought a new kind of tension that we couldn't handle in our usual way. She seemed to almost control us. The locker room after practice lost its towel-slapping good-time feeling. A lot of people think jocks are immature, but I think there's something hotly primal about being naked and sweaty in a locker room, the place all steamed up from hot showers, after having sprinted for three hours. I'm never happier than I am then. But with Thalia there everything changed. I got the feeling she didn't like to undress in front of us. Yet, out of pride, she paraded around, displaying her body parts as if to make clear that no lesbians were gonna cow her. We all averted our eyes. Not that I wanted to look. I didn't. A heterosexual energy, the dangerous kind, wafted off her like strong perfume.

Most of us cooled down after practice, pulled on our pants, joked about dinner. Basketball practice launched me into the rest of my life, as if it was the source and everything else flowed from there. But for Thalia, the locker room was a place of transition. She had a routine as amazing as a Dr. Jekyll and Mr. Hyde act. As she applied make-up and pulled on nylon stockings, she transformed from basketball animal to Phi Beta Pi lady. She often shaved her legs in the locker room, slowly and carefully, as if to show how much others of us needed to do the same. By the time she left the locker room, this basketball powerhouse had become a graceful swan. The woman was smooth.

So the locker room was a lot quieter that year. We just showered and went off to dinner. Team jokes from last year fell flat and no new ones arose. Something about Thalia made me feel young and inadequate. Only Stella seemed to be at ease with her, making small conversation as if she didn't notice Thalia's cool response. Thalia was too southern polite not to speak when spoken to, but she didn't want to talk, that was clear. We all saw that and didn't try. Except Stella.

I admired Stella more than anyone on the team. She was so solid. Jackie told me that Stella went to church every Sunday morning. She struck you as beautiful when you first saw her because of her carriage, but on closer inspection her face was rather plain. At first I didn't get why she, a poised and cultured black woman from L.A., was with Coach Montgomery, a thirty-five-year-old white woman from the Midwest. Coach had broad even features and a jaunty smile—*when* she smiled, which wasn't often. In a way, though black and white, Stella and Montgomery looked a bit alike. The big difference besides color was Stella's elegance and Montgomery's jock walk. The two of them were pretty discreet because much as I tried, I never saw anything pass between them during practices. They must have been scared at times. I sure was, and I didn't have a job to protect. I privately drew from Stella's sure confidence and from Montgomery's courage to live and love as she pleased. Without speaking an intimate word with either of these two women, I considered them my lesbian mentors. As something nameless thickened between Jackie and myself, I kept my eyes trained on Montgomery and Stella, looking for a signal, the go-ahead, something in their plain, forward moving faces that would tell me what my next move should be.

On the night of our third home game I jogged out onto the court with my team, so happy I thought I could die right then and be satisfied with my life. Jackie and I had finally started up our love affair. A sweetness coursed through my limbs, making me feel like an Olympic hurdler flying over life's obstacles with perfect elegance. On top of that our team was winning. Our record was a tremendous 7–0. Thalia's family had donated brand-new uniforms to the team (she had been complaining about how ghastly ugly the old ones were), so we looked pretty sharp too. When we lined up for lay-ups the school band blasted into action. Even the cheerleading squad pranced onto center court and whipped their pompons around. Understand that the band and cheerleaders did not attend women's games until we were on a winning streak, until there was glory to be reaped. I wasn't bitter though. I loved it. I even loved the hordes of fraternity boys that packed the gym. The night was fine.

We were playing North Carolina State, and we held a decent lead during most of the first half. I sat back on the bench and watched Jackie speed up and down the court. The movement of each muscle was a precious sight to me.

Shortly before halftime Montgomery benched Thalia to give her a breather and put in Carson. Suddenly the game turned around. North Carolina State broke our lead and then, in a quick ten minutes, proceeded to fast break to an eight-point lead. Seconds before halftime, North Carolina State got the ball again, and went for the fast break. The buzzer sounded and the guard tipped the ball in for a lay-up. The official called the basket good. Montgomery lunged onto the court toward the ref, screaming that the basket sunk after the buzzer.

The ref slapped his hand to the back of his head, pointed at Montgomery, and called a technical foul on her. The crowd went crazy because Montgomery was right. That girl wasn't anywhere near the basket when the buzzer sounded. Someone pulled Montgomery back to the bench, and we lined up at half court while the player toed the line for her free throw. Carson was kicking the floor like a mad bull because she knew everyone would interpret our sudden slide to be a result of Montgomery putting her in and taking Thalia out. The North Carolina State player made her shot.

After a good talking-to at halftime we trotted back out onto the court and warmed up. Then Montgomery did something that surprised us all—she started Carson instead of Thalia. I figured she thought Carson was losing her confidence and put her in to let her know she wasn't to blame for the score. Montgomery always emphasized that we were a team, that one woman couldn't make or break anything. A nervous silence fell on the gym as the ten players took positions for the tip-off. A cold sweat saturated the air. I could see Carson's mouth working and would have thought she was praying if I didn't know better. Jackie wiped her hands on her hips and glanced at me. I felt instant warmth again. The ref held the ball up and glanced around the circle. He hesitated as two players suddenly traded places. Then, just as he bent his knees to make the toss, a male voice in the bleachers erupted out of the perfect silence. "Bench the dyke! Play Thalia Peterson."

For a split second everyone in the gym was stunned. The air felt yellow and still. Even the ref, who stood between the two centers with the ball balanced on his fingertips, stepped back and squinted at the stands. Then a gurgling of fraternity laughter eased some people's discomfort and the ref tossed the ball.

Something turned sour for me in that moment at halftime against North Carolina State. Everyone knew the fraternity boy meant Carson, but I knew that he also meant Stella and Montgomery, Jackie and myself. The raw hatred in his voice felt like a boot stomping on a tender green shoot.

We lost that game and the next one too. Every time I stepped into the big, silent gym for practice, I heard an echo of that boy's voice. Sometimes, for a flashing second, I could even see the group of fraternity boys in the stands, jeering, knowing. Montgomery and Stella were no help anymore; they were as indicted as I was. Jackie and I had our first fight that week.

Looking back, I think it's a miracle we ever won any games. So many of us were in some stage of coming out, no one really comfortable, none of us able to say "lesbian" without cringing. We were scared, we were in love, we were all little bundles of explosive passion. Sometimes this energy drove us to victory on the court, other times we crumbled under it.

By midseason Jackie and I were solid. We were crazy for each other, but love isn't everything and we fought a lot. She didn't know what she was doing messing with a white girl and I didn't know what I was doing messing with any girl at all. Our common ground lay in the realm of ideals and primal loves and fears, but our earthbound experiences were different enough to make us both crazy. We carried on just the same.

After the North Carolina State game, Montgomery began switching around the starting line-up. It's not like she substituted one starter for another (say, Carson for Thalia), but out of the top six players she tried different combinations and often Carson was in there. Sometimes Thalia was not.

Mixing up the starting line-up too much might not be smart basketball (though in this case it might have been), but it sure made me like Montgomery. I don't really know why she did it, but I suspect she saw it as a morale issue. She probably noticed how that boy's remark registered on some of our young faces. Maybe she knew she had some power to erase the imprint of that boot. With me she was right, I secretly drew from her strength, but the morale of the rest of the team sagged. When Thalia didn't start she lounged on the bench as if it were a settee, as if she was entertaining in a drawing room and hadn't the faintest interest in the game, and when Montgomery put her in she gave only seventy-five percent. If Montgomery started her, however, Thalia gave her all. The insult to Montgomery, the idea that she could be manipulated by Thalia's insolence, infuriated me. I was glad when Montgomery started her less and less often. A rumor circulated that Thalia's parents offered a large donation to the Women's Intercollegiate Fund on the behind-closed-doors stipulation that Thalia be reinstated as a permanent first stringer. I don't know if this was true, but people swore it was. Someone knew someone who knew someone who worked in Dean Roper's office. She'd heard the offer. I believed the story more than I disbelieved it.

Carson saw the changing line-up as an opportunity to re-establish her position on the team. Her attitude improved. She kept her mouth shut and played ball like it was a matter of life and death. At the same time Carson became more and more out about her lesbianism. She thought everyone else should come out as well. "A bunch of fucking closet dykes," she semi-joked at me and Jackie one night in the library. She took that boy's word like it was a piece of clay and fashioned her own meaning out of it. I cringed and quickly looked over my shoulder to see if anyone was within earshot. Jackie just shrugged. "With Montgomery and Stella we're talking about a job," she said. Yeah, I thought, and with me we're talking about fear. Jackie didn't want to come out and I happily hid behind her wishes. So for lesbians on the team that just left the jealousy-à-trois, as we called them, three women who had not yet managed to come out even to themselves but were involved in a triangle of jealousy complicated, in my opinion, by a lack of sex. Of course there were the four definitely straight women on the team: Susan Thurmond, Amanda Severson, Kathy Jones, and Thalia Peterson. Somehow we were more and more aware of who was who. Somehow that individual clarity seemed to dissolve our team clarity.

One day, near the end of the season, Montgomery came into practice a half hour late. Her face was tight and pasty looking. "Put on sweats," she ordered. "Dean Roper is coming to talk with you.

Meet back here." She disappeared into her office.

When we returned to the gym, we sat on the bleachers. Roper came in with a Father-Knows-Best smile on his face. "Carson," he said, forcing a twinkle to his eye, "why don't you come on in first."

"What?" Thalia kept saying, her voice pitched high. "I don't get it."

Thalia was not a good actress. It was obvious that she was the only one who *did* get it.

Five minutes later, Carson came out glaring. "It's the Inquisition," she mumbled, throwing herself on a bench.

"Go on and get dressed, Carson," Roper ordered, knowing an agitator when he saw one.

I expected Carson to challenge Roper, at least by hesitating before obeying, but perhaps she realized the safety of the rest of us hinged on not exciting him further. Carson left and Roper called in Stella, who strode before the dean like a gazelle leading a turtle.

One by one Roper called us into Montgomery's office. Except for Carson, each came back out and sat on the bench with the rest of us. No one spoke a word. Finally, second from last, my turn came. I was surprised to see Coach sitting next to the big oak desk in her own office. I couldn't believe that she had had to sit through each of the interviews. Roper sat at Montgomery's desk. He leaned forward, no longer smiling. "We've had some problems on the team I understand." He spoke slowly. I could tell that despite some discomfort he was savoring every moment of this scandal. "Many of the women I've spoken to have felt unsafe because of the lesbianism on the team. What about you?"

"I feel safe."

"Are you a lesbian?" Roper looked as if he had tasted the word. I glanced involuntarily at Montgomery, expecting her to protect me, but her eyes were blank. I stared at her folded hands realizing she had been forced to sit through even the interrogation of Stella. My eyes moved from her hands to her chest. She wasn't breathing. Suddenly I wanted to protect her. My mind raced, frantically searching for the right response. I thought of Jackie, of Stella and Montgomery. I looked Roper squarely in the face and remained utterly silent.

He sighed, "I can't force you to speak young lady. We'll get to the bottom of this one way or another. Whichever side you're on, you may be sure it will be straightened out."

When I went back into the gym the whole team looked at me and I knew they were trying to read my face, to guess what I had said. No one moved, waiting for Roper to call in the last of us—Thalia Peterson. Roper was not a shrewd man. In fact, after this slip I knew he was downright stupid. He never did call Thalia. He left by a back door and Montgomery came to tell us to shower and go to dinner.

"Okay, no one is leaving the locker room," Kathy Jones said after practice two days later.

"What's going on?" Carson stood, pants unzipped and one shoe in hand, ready to fight.

"Be mellow, McDuffy," Amanda Severson warned.

Susan Thurmond was suddenly at Amanda's and Kathy's side. Three of the four straight women stood in a block. Thalia had her back turned and was shoveling her brush, clothes and blow dryer into her gym bag, fast. She grabbed the bag and headed for the door without even brushing her hair.

"Where're you going, Peterson?" Kathy said. Since when was Thalia called Peterson?

Thalia tossed her blond hair, ran fingers through the top. "This has nothing to do with me."

"Oh, I think it may have everything to do with you."

A First Lady smile. "I'm real busy. Gotta go."

"I bet you could spare five minutes." This from Amanda walking toward Thalia. Thalia sat on the bench, a good distance away from the rest of us.

"What's the deal?" Carson struck her butchest stance, facing off with the straight girls.

"Mellow, McDuffy."

"Don't tell me what to be, Severson." Carson stepped forward, slitting her eyes.

"So what's going on?" Jackie finally said, the only sensible tone of voice so far.

"We thought we should all talk," Amanda said. I understood the first "we" to mean the straight women. "Look, we still have a chance to make it to the playoffs. And this . . . this bullshit about lesbians on the team, well . . . ."

"Fuck yourself!" Carson screamed. "You all can just go fuck yourselves."

Kathy Jones lunged for Carson, then stopped half an inch from her face. "Shut up, McDuffy. You ain't got a chip on your shoulder, you got a block of wood so big you can't see your own ugly face in the mirror."

Carson went for her throat. A split second later Jackie was there, wrangling Carson's hands off Kathy. I tried to arrest her kicking legs. At the same time Amanda subdued Kathy.

"For goodness sakes, *listen*," Amanda screamed.

We all turned when we heard Thalia say, in a near-growl, "Let me out of here." But Susan Thurmond blocked the door.

Shit, what was this? The straight girls getting ready to pound the shit out of us? Threaten or blackmail us? I started to sweat all over again.

"Go ahead, Amanda," Kathy said, her eyes impaling Carson.

"Kathy, Susan and I wanted to tell you, well, we wanted to talk. None of us three gave any names, okay? None of us told Roper anything. We didn't say whether we were straight or whatever." Amanda sat on the bench and tears flowed into her eyes. "Geez, we used to be a *team*. We've got to pull together. Look, we *are* pulling together. See, that's why we haven't heard anything more from Roper. Don't you get it? He got no information. *None*."

"You mean none of you all said you were straight?" This was me, slow as always, taking it in.

"No. None of us said anything to that sleaze bag. What about the rest of you?"

"I didn't give him a clue."

"Nope."

"I just told him I didn't know and didn't give a shit either."

"I told him I was a lesbian," Carson said slowly, looking at her feet. "I said I had no idea if anyone else was."

"You take the hard road every time," Kathy Jones almost whispered.

"I just tell the truth." Carson tried to harden, but looked soft for once in her life.

"That's everyone but you, Thalia." We all turned to the end of the bench where Thalia sat, her face hot and red. We watched her muster all the aristocratic poise she could, but it wasn't much. For the first time in the year I'd known her, I saw the woman lose it. Her hands were shaking, with anger I thought. Thalia had assumed her power in this situation. The past few days she had been looking more serene than usual, beauteous, as if a struggle had finally been resolved. It had never occurred to her that she would be sacrificed for the triumph of sisterhood.

"Thalia," pressed Amanda, "what did *you* tell Dean Roper?"

"He didn't call me in."

"Right. Then obviously you had already spoken to him."

Thalia stood and managed to say, "I have no idea what any of you are talking about." Those narrow eyes nearly crossed.

We sat and stared in silence at her straight posture, her composed face with the high cheekbones, her long graceful arms. Suddenly I saw a long line of stern, puritan women, severely beautiful and rich women, stacking up behind her as if she were in a house of mirrors. Mothers, grandmothers and great-grandmothers, all of them echoing, "I have no idea what any of you are talking about . . . I have no idea what any of you are talking about . . . I have no idea . . ."

We partied that night. Me, Jackie, Susan, Amanda, Kathy, Carson, even the jealousy-à-trois. Everyone except for Stella, Coach and, of course, Thalia, gathered in Jackie's room and hashed over everything we'd missed this year during Thalia Peterson's reign of terror. We died laughing at every story, rocking in our relief at being safe. We raked Thalia over the coals, tearing her apart hair by hair, gesture by gesture. We were cruel.

But we softened as the night wore on and eventually crossed over that magic line into the dark blue waters of early morning. We left Thalia behind like a wrecked ship. Useless. History. Slowly and carefully we began telling stories from last year, only now elaborating on the jock, punch-line versions to fill in nuances, shades of meaning, our feelings. Some of us told our coming-out stories, our fears of others on the team finding out. We spoke, our voices tentative, about how much the team meant to us, how each woman was an experience in our lives we could never replace. Outside the single window of Jackie's dorm room daylight permeated the sky. I switched off the desk lamp. Even Carson, slumped on the corner of Jackie's bed, said in her husky voice, "Yeah, I guess I blew it in the locker room. We're all pulling together. Yeah, we're all pulling our share, aren't we?"

"Yeah," I said. I felt as if I finally understood the source of brilliance in a perfectly executed defense, in a flawless three-on-two fast break, in a full-court press when every team member was exactly where she was supposed to be.

We did not make it to the playoffs, Carson did not make the Eastern Division All-Star team (though Thalia did), and Jackie and I didn't make it through to the end of the year. She began seeing another woman on the team, finally bringing out one corner of the jealous triangle (which allowed the remaining two to collapse together in yet another torrid basketball romance). Naturally I was devastated and mushed through my final exams like a rain-soaked puppy, stupid, sloppy, miserable and eager for the tiniest show of kindness. On the night before my last exam the phone rang. When I answered, Jackie's voice filled the receiver. I hadn't talked to her in three weeks and was so overwhelmed by her presence in my ear that I didn't even listen to what she said.

"You okay?" she repeated. "I just wanted to say hello."

"I miss you," I blurted.

"I know babe," she sighed. I could feel her sorrow too, and that helped. "But we had a good year anyway, didn't we?"

"Yeah," I said, crying and then sobbing. In spite of everything it had been the best year of my life.

THE PLACE BEFORE LANGUAGE

PICTURE ME in my Class A National Park Service uniform: the polished-to-a-luster shoes, the green trousers with the razor-sharp crease, the belt with the embossed pine cones, the short green jacket with the shiny badge and brass buttons, and the wide-brimmed Smokey the Bear hat. The whole bit. You see a woman who can name every wildflower on Mount Rainier, who has climbed at least eight major peaks, who knows the secret life of glaciers.

You think you see a woman in control. But really you see a femme at heart hoping to find relief in a butch getup. My summer job as a ranger on Mount Rainier in Washington State had not stopped my raging fantasies about murdering Donna's new girlfriend. Graphic pictures—of my hands around her neck, of my green Park Service truck colliding with her bulk—lit the dark recesses of my mind like little nuclear explosions. I couldn't stop them. I didn't want to.

She—the new girlfriend—was dog ugly and had a personality that lurked in dark corners. She looked like she needed a vigorous trot in country air. Near the end of our ten years together

Donna had called me a bulldozer, and compared to this beige, papery moth, I suppose I did come across forcefully. I never denied being a high-maintenance girlfriend. I knew I wasn't an easy person, but then I didn't think that "easy" was what Donna was after.

Yet it wasn't my bright obsession with violence that disturbed me. If I'd had the chance to act on my fantasies, I don't doubt that I would have. What really bothered me was the feeling that my grasp on everything I'd always known to be true was slipping, that a vital part of my brain had shaken loose and was rattling around in my head like useless machinery.

You see, until last summer, I had believed in the power of language. I lived with the conviction that everything could be said. Words were life's cradle, the way to name, shape, hold, and, yes, control one's world. I had always believed that as I sharpened my verbal skills so too would my world view come more crisply into focus. Language to me was like a massive database where one filed away experience, relentlessly, day after day. Even as I was living each moment, I was assigning words to it, writing it, wrapping it up in a neat package of verbiage.

This word castle crumbled when Donna dumped me. I felt hollow and formless as I started the summer on Mount Rainier. I searched and searched for sentences, even simple phrases, to house my feelings, to use as handholds. I couldn't find them. All I had were visions—of human roadkill, of strangulation—visions that burned in my gut like forest fires, hot and out of control.

Visions and this uniform.

I was stationed for the summer at Sunrise, a set of cabins just above the tree line on the east side of the mountain. When I arrived in mid-June, a roommate named Beth had already moved in. "I've taken the bottom bunk," she said, "but if you prefer it we can draw straws."

"I'm usually a bottom," I answered to amuse myself, "but I need a change. I'll take the top."

In those first couple weeks I hardly used the bunk at all. I started almost every evening by trying to write Donna a letter, but could never even begin it. I couldn't sleep either, so I spent the nights haunting the trails around Sunrise. Up there the mountain was so close it filled half the sky, and even when the moon wasn't out, the stars were so abundant and the mountain so bright with glaciers that I could go anywhere without a flashlight. I would climb out to the end of Sourdough Ridge or explore the Silver Forest, a shadowy grove of smooth silver snags left over from a fire long ago. The meadows were full of columbine, aster, paintbrush, phlox, heather, monkey flower, and lupine, and, where the snow was just melting, glacier lilies, their colors rich and magical in the starlight. Sometimes I would hike out to Frozen Lake or down to Sunrise Lake.

These night prowls provided no insights, no answers, no inspirations and no relief from wanting to murder Lurking Dog. I felt eclipsed by the massive glowing mountain, as if I didn't exist at all against its grand backdrop. And yet, looking back, I see that those hikes were a kind of boot camp of the soul. I was getting ready.

On the first of July, after two weeks on the job, I led a large crowd of park visitors from the Visitor Center down to the Emmons Glacier viewpoint to deliver one of my talks. It was a cold, blustery day, the air metallic with negative ions. Under my woolen Class As I wore long underwear, yet half the crowd wore shorts and T-shirts—vacation clothes. No matter that they were vacationing in alpine terrain.

I loved that uniform. It made me someone else, someone fortunate, someone desirable. On the way to the viewpoint, a retired couple asked me to join them later for coffee and home-baked cookies in their RV down in the White River campground. The woman nearly pinched my cheek. I was their symbol of perfect wholesomeness. Then a young man accompanied by a huge family plied me with questions about how I got my job. I was *his* symbol of perfect independence. I didn't tell him that he didn't have a snowball's chance in hell of supporting his four kids and wife on a ranger's salary.

I enjoyed the interest these folks had in me, but it was a party of three teenagers that caught and held my attention. Older kids usually weren't interested in ranger-led walks, except as opportunities to harass. The uniform sometimes provokes people who are hungry to get revenge on authority figures. Rangers can't give out bad grades like teachers or arrest like cops, so we're easy prey. The week before I'd had to ask a group of lesbians, who were sitting on the delicate tundra as they ate their lunch, to please move to the picnic area. I may as well have been a cop in the nation's most corrupt police force, or maybe best friends with Newt Gingrich, for how belligerently they responded. I only wanted to protect the tundra.

These kids seemed different though—too vital to be petty about perceived authority. The girl had long blond hair so thin and babysoft her prominent ears jutted out from its curtain. She clung to a hunk of a guy whose brow, nose and jaw were all square. His long bare legs were gorgeously muscled and lightly furred. If he hadn't worn big clunky plastic glasses that looked like they belonged on his dad he'd have been excessively handsome. The third kid wore his light brown shoulder-length hair climber fashion, in whiteboy dreads. Rather than shorts, he wore long fleece pants and two flannel shirts, the top one buttoned two buttonholes out of sync. He had the smoothest skin, nearly beardless, and full, dark red lips. While the girl and bigger boy groped one another, their friend seemed to sulk.

We arrived at the viewpoint but there wasn't a view. For days like these—most days—there was a big photo of the mountain in a big display under glass. I began giving my talk, pointing out interesting facts about Mount Rainier.

Next to the uniform, my favorite part of the job was the title: Interpretive Ranger. My job was to interpret nature for the park visitors. Sometimes I pictured myself crouching down to place my ear close to a wildflower, nodding attentively, then standing and telling the park visitors, "She says the best moment of the year is when she pushes that first green nose of her stem up through the still partially frozen soil. . ." Or, when an avalanche spilled down the face of Rainier and the rumbling carried all the way to our ears at Sunrise, I fantasized waving my arms, screaming, "She said get out! Everybody move now! Back to Seattle! She's gonna blow!"

Of course that wasn't what Interpretive Ranger meant, so I just did my job. Naming tree species wasn't a problem. I knew the history of who'd first climbed Rainier and by what route. I also knew the defining features of each geological era. But really. How do you interpret a mountain? Had anyone *seen* its molten core? Did anyone *really* know how mountains formed? For that matter, if clouds envelop a mountain so that no one can see it, does that mountain really exist?

Okay, the last is a trite question, but one I had to answer constantly.

To the New Yorker in this morning's group, the answer was no. At one point during my talk I made the mistake of gesturing in the direction of the invisible mountain.

"Miss! Miss!" A balding fellow, whose Bronx accent was obvious even in that one word, waved his hand in the air as if we were in a classroom. I paused.

"How're we supposed to call this a vacation when we can't see no mountain?"

I smiled sympathetically at the man from the Bronx, as if he'd been joking, and continued explaining about the Ice Age, how the big Emmons Glacier was advancing a foot a year, the difference between river-carved and glacier-carved valleys. As I spoke I tried not to watch the bigger teenage boy who stood behind the girl, gently bumping his pelvis into her behind. I sympathized with the other boy who stood with them scowling.

In the last part of my talk I told about the first woman to climb Mount Rainier, Fay Fuller. As soon as I said her name my coworker and roommate, Beth, stepped out from behind the trees dressed as Fay Fuller—long skirt, walking stick, nineteenth century lace-up boots—and took over the rap. As always, the visitors ate up the drama.

I stepped aside and pretended to listen to Beth a.k.a. Fay Fuller's story as I watched the blond girl reach behind herself and squeeze her hands between her body and the big boy's. You didn't have to be a rocket scientist to know she was stroking his—surely hard—penis. She eventually swiveled to face him and they murmured softly to one another, still bumping gently, while Beth continued her talk in perfect ladylike nineteenth-century enunciation.

I wasn't too fond of my roommate. She could make a batch of cookies, put them in a cookie jar, then eat one, maybe two, a day. I couldn't keep myself from stealing her cookies and never stole fewer than five or six at a time. I hated that she knew I was stealing her cookies and never said anything.

Soon Beth leaned on her walking stick and headed back up the trail saying, "And so goes, my friends, another climb . . ." which was my cue. I was supposed to jump in with, "Shall we follow

Fay back up to the Visitor Center?" On the way back I'd pretend to spontaneously notice nature, like the variety of cones on the trees or the network of marmot tunneling, but today I'd fixated on the two sexually aroused teenagers and their miserably excluded friend, so I missed my cue. The park visitors thought the talk was over and began wandering back up the trail without my guidance.

The man from the Bronx, his wife and the three teenagers remained. "You don't understand," the man said, poking a finger at my chest. "We drove, you hear me, we drove from New York state." He raised his eyebrows and lowered his head as if he were looking over the top of his glasses, only he wasn't wearing any. I understood he wanted an explanation about the mountain.

I looked over my shoulder at Rainier, hoping she might oblige by emerging. Sometimes just the peak appeared, seeming to float on the clouds. Today I looked into a complete canvas of bright gray, like a single-color modern art painting in which some people, like me, actually saw a mountain. I was supposed to smile sympathetically at the visitors from the Bronx and say, "I wish we could snap our fingers and make the clouds disappear but we can't." Instead I barked, "Well, you missed it."

"Of course we missed it," the wife said. "Don't pester the girl, Norm."

"What I'm saying is," Norm shifted from one foot to the other and then back again, "this is our only vacation."

I heard the three kids snickering. I looked at the delicate boy who pressed his ruddy lips together and averted his eyes.

"So?" the wife said. "The ranger is supposed to be able to disappear the clouds for you? Don't be an idiot, Norm."

"You don't get it, do you?" he asked, finally leaving me and following his wife up the trail. "My whole life I've wanted to see the mountains in the West. . . ."

I waited a moment before beginning my walk back up to the Visitor Center so I wouldn't have to talk anymore with the New Yorkers.

"So, like, what's the weather report?" It was the excluded boy. He had beautiful green eyes. Behind him his friends leaned against the glass-covered display, again stroking one another. I wanted to tell him that the blond girl had made a very bad choice. She should be fondling him. "More of the same," I said, not wanting to disappoint with the information that a storm was due. They should have known themselves. All you had to do was touch your hair and feel the crackle.

"That guy who wanted to see the mountain," said the boy. "He wouldn't even look at it if it was out. He'd, like, take a picture and leave."

I smiled. It was true.

The boy looked at the ground as he said, "I think it's more beautiful *not* seeing the mountain. Just knowing it's there."

I put a hand on his shoulder, ran it down his thin, flanneled arm, then withdrew it quickly, embarrassed. He looked me full-on for the first time, batting those big, beautiful green eyes.

Walking back up the trail alone, I thought he'd made my day, maybe my whole week.

Three days later Jack Keeney came into the Visitor Center in the late afternoon. I was using a pointer on the big table relief map to describe the five best hikes out of Sunrise, my last visitor talk of the day.

"Speak to you when you're done here," he said.

Jack Keeney wasn't my boss. He supervised the more prestigious backcountry ranger staff. Everyone answered to Jack Keeney, though, whether he had any authority over you or not.

When I got over to the back country office Jack was on the phone. He motioned for me to hold on, finished up his call, then said, "Uh, Terry?"

"Tracy," I said. I'd been here for three weeks. I'd heard plenty from and about Jack in that time. He was sort of a legend on the mountain. Clearly, I hadn't made a big impression on him.

"Sorry. Tracy, three kids are missing on the mountain. Two boys, seventeen and eighteen, and a girl, sixteen, started climbing from White River two days ago. They were expected back at their camp by late afternoon yesterday. They never arrived. Did you see any climbers from the VC day before yesterday?"

I'd seen them. The Sunrise Visitor Center has enormous glass windows facing the mountain, and from there climbers look like tiny strings of ants. With strong binoculars you can make out their ropes, ice axes and fleece hats. Two mornings ago I had seen three dots and had been impressed because they were climbing quickly—and also because no one should have been on the mountain. The clouds, full and still, had turned that polished gray color that meant storm. The Park Service had put out an advisory against climbing.

I told Jack everything I'd seen through the binoculars, trying to guess accurately the climbers' exact location at the time. Then I asked, "What did they look like, do you know?"

"Blond girl. One guy big, glasses. The other skinny, long hair."

A blackness spread behind my eyes, that hammering why, why, why feeling. Those ridiculous jutting ears. The gorgeous legs. That sweet boy's voice telling me how the mountain was more beautiful when you couldn't see it but knew it was there. Those soulful green eyes. He hadn't said anything to me about climbing, but he had asked about the weather. I told Jack, "I think they were hanging around Sunrise the day before they climbed. They came on one of my Emmons Glacier viewpoint walks."

He looked slightly interested. "Did they look like they knew what they were doing? Or would you know?"

Jerk. What did he know about what I knew? He turned away, not even waiting for my answer. So I didn't give him one. They *had* looked like climbers, but they were so young, so hormonally overwhelmed.

Back in the tiny kitchen of our cabin, I moved around Beth, trying to warm some leftover pasta. She was carefully washing three leaves of lettuce, patting dry a potato for baking, trimming the fat off a tiny steak. After she cooked and ate all that, she would wash her dishes, put on tea water, set a cookie on a plate, read a chapter of a book . . . I couldn't stand to watch tonight. So after unsuccessfully trying to eat the pasta, I went next door to the Visitor Center, now closed to visitors, where staff was hanging out in front of the big fireplace. So far I'd avoided socializing with other employees. The Park Service attracts a lot of born-again Christians and military folks. I'm not sure how the first group gets a leg up, but veterans get a load of extra points in the hiring system, so unless they have glaring deficiencies, they can get jobs pretty easily. I liked everyone well enough but wasn't so sure they'd like me if they knew me. My roommate had already reacted pretty strongly to my short bookshelf. It held only ten volumes, but each one packed a good lesbian punch. "Whoa," she'd said, backing off as if the books put out a bad smell. I didn't say anything, nor did I come out to her. I didn't really care if she shared what she'd learned from my books with other staff. I wanted the isolation.

Tonight, though, I needed to know about those kids, so I stood in front of the big fire in the Visitor Center, drank coffee, and listened with my co-workers to Jack, who was next door in the ranger station communicating with the search-and-rescue team on the shortwave radio. Occasionally, I put my head out the door.

Night had swept in around the mountain along with a stiff wind and spitting rain. Up there it would be snow. Back inside I tried to make myself useful by throwing fresh logs on the fire and refilling people's coffee cups.

We all listened to Jack barking out commands over the radio as if he were the voice of God. All the lesser rangers loved talking about Jack, though no one dared gossip about him openly. He was too grand for that. Instead, I heard soft-spoken references to his tour in Vietnam, accounts of mountain rescues he'd orchestrated singlehandedly, even whispered tributes to his marriage. Barbara and Jack, I'd heard, shared the ingredients of a perfect relationship: a love of the outdoors, a clear decision not to have children, a simple close-to-the-bone existence. Barbara, according to male rangers, was the ideal woman, both gorgeous and able to keep up. The old-timer staff on Rainier spoke of Jack proudly, as if his accomplishments were their own.

I dropped a log on my toe when I heard a woman's voice on the radio. I immediately recognized it as Elise Sawyer's.

The Mount Fremont lookout, where Elise had been stationed every summer for the past ten years, was primarily a fire tower, but it was also positioned for relaying messages around to the other side of the mountain. I remembered hearing Jack say how Elise had never missed a single fire. She was more dependable than any man he knew. Most fire lookout people had been replaced by patrol planes, but as long as she wanted it, Jack had said, Elise Sawyer could have her job.

Her alliance with the boys made me wary of her. Yet, sitting among these John Denver-loving, born-again types, the husky female voice in my ear was as luring as a tongue.

I'd met Elise once, at the same time I first met Jack Keeney, nearly a month ago at the beginning-of-the-season cookout for seasonal employees. Elise had looked like the only prospective dyke in the crowd, so after getting my food I followed her to the shade of a Douglas fir, where she joined a tall, auburn-haired woman and a man who looked like an army sergeant. Elise looked the man dead in the eye, without smiling, and shook his hand firmly, saying, "Jack. Good to see you." Only then did she turn to the woman and say, "How're you doing, Barbara?" All three of them ignored me. I could have left, but then I'd have to try to break into some other conversation. At least here I had the chance of meeting a dyke. So I introduced myself. Balancing my limp paper plate of ribs, corn on the cob, and green salad in one hand, I shook their hands with my other. Elise Sawyer was less than friendly, almost sulky, but I liked, at least admired, Barbara and Jack. Besides her bronze hair, Barbara had formidable cheekbones and a mouth that looked vulnerable, as if she were ready to kiss someone. Jack had a crew cut, big dimples, and a lean, muscled body. Together they broadcast a feeling of capability, like they were a team more than a marriage. I imagined them having athletic sex.

As the conversation stumbled along, tensely, I thought, I tried to make significant eye contact with Elise. She appeared not just uninterested in me, but almost hostile. I got the feeling she wanted Jack and Barbara to herself. Well, excuse me. I wasn't trying to flirt with her or anything. Could a little lesbian camaraderie hurt? I left to get more ribs, thinking that this summer was going to be even lonelier than I had anticipated.

I had not spoken with Elise since those few words at the cookout a month ago. Tonight her rugged voice coming over the radio waves stirred me. Her competence, her complete control of the situation, impressed me. I wished I could help, but my climbing experience didn't matter because women were not considered for search-and-rescue teams.

I remained quiet for as long as I could while my fellow Park

Service employees spoke softly about the reckless climbers. According to some folks camped at the White River campground who had spoken with them, the kids had come all the way from Wisconsin to climb and they had to be home at the end of the week. They'd known about the storm advisory, but they'd decided to take their chances.

My co-workers clucked and shook their heads.

"Foolish kids..."

"Taxpayer's money..."

"... as if you can just up and do whatever you want."

"They'd only wanted to climb the mountain," I finally said, thinking about how they'd driven all the way from Wisconsin. They'd wanted it that badly.

Six faces turned toward me, adjusting to my comment, probably judging me now. I sighed, stood up, poured more coffee. I found myself respecting those kids, who'd ignored good judgment, and hating these folks around me, who doled out their lives like treats that had to last a long time. I got the sense these people wanted the kids to get their due. Probably they didn't want them to die, but maybe lose a finger or two, suffer the extreme symptoms of hypothermia.

My restlessness became unbearable so I went back to my cabin where Beth was reading a book and nibbling a cookie. I pulled on a sweatshirt, down parka and my Gortex suit, then set out in the thick mist and light rain, treading the mile out to Frozen Lake where the trail forked in three directions. One went up to Burrough's Mountain, one down to Berkeley Park and the third over to the lookout tower on Mount Fremont. I climbed in the opposite direction of the lookout tower. The dense clouds made the night black and cold. Patches of snow still nestled against the leeward slopes.

As I climbed the rain let up but the frozen mist engulfed me. I could barely see the trail at my feet and definitely couldn't see anything ahead. I felt acutely aware of the warmth of my own body, the only warmth for miles around, and missed Donna. I wondered where she was tonight and briefly pictured her stroking the pasty skin of Lurking Dog. My muscles spasmed with the desire to do violence.

I considered wandering deeper and deeper into this lush fog and never re-emerging. Donna would miss me then. She counted on getting the chance to talk things out eventually. As if you could talk out the betrayal of a ten-year relationship. I could disappear like those kids. Donna would have to live with the absence of me, the total, absolute absence of me.

In June, after packing my car for the summer, I had stopped by her house before driving up to Rainier. I hadn't seen or spoken with her in a month, ever since she'd started up with Lurking Dog. I was leaving and I wanted her to feel it, see my packed car, know that I was not only running from something but going to something. Which was why on that late spring day I wore my uniform.

As I pulled up in front of her house I saw a brand new lipstick-red Miata, too new to even have plates, parked in her driveway. Donna, all five feet and eight inches of her, was stepping out of the driver's seat. She wore Levi's—30/32—and a khaki buttondown shirt. Her tousled sandy hair made her look relaxed, easy with herself, and she was well-tanned, though it was not yet summer. She always managed to look elegantly casual, as if she'd just thrown herself together. Her nails were always perfectly manicured, clear pink with little white halfmoons at the cuticles.

"Tracy!" she said, appropriately surprised. She regained her composure and added, "Hey, you look hot in that uniform."

The way she admired my uniform took it away from me somehow, made it more hers than mine.

"Where'd you get the Miata?" I asked touching its red paint.

"I work hard. I deserve it."

"No one said you didn't. It's just . . . not like you." I guessed it was part of the mid-life crisis that included dumping me.

She put out a hand to shake. Shake! Like we were business acquaintances. Still I gave her my hand, probably because of some hope deep in my body that she'd hold it to her lips, murmur she wanted me back, ask would I have her. She definitely *shook* my hand, didn't hold it, and let go. I looked over my shoulder at Mount Rainier, visible from the city today, and comforted myself by knowing the mountain was mine, not hers, on account of my job and the uniform. The mountain loomed like the biggest, coldest bodyguard.

"So I'm off," I said and nodded my head out at the mountain, "for the summer."

"I'm glad you came to say goodbye." She used that soft fakey voice she used to use in front of our couple counselor. The little lines around her eyes, the ones I loved, streaked out across her temples. Her smile looked vicious.

"Where's Lurking Dog?" I asked.

Donna looked confused. Of course she didn't know who Lurking Dog was. She said, "I was hoping we could talk sometime."

"Maybe next fall," I said.

"Ten years," she said. "Then total silence. It doesn't make sense."

Did I miss something? Had I been the one to leave her?

"Okay," she patronized softly. "You take your time. I can wait."

I'd worn the uniform for authority, for control over the situation. Now it felt like a foil for her ease. By the time I left, I felt like a cop, or worse, like a schoolgirl in her safety patrol tunic. When I got in my car and drove away, she was already entering her house, not even feeling my loss enough to watch the tailend of my car down the street.

Tonight, as I reached the top of Burrough's Mountain and climbed out of the fog, I realized that as much as I was worried about those three kids, I also envied them. I'd tried so hard all these years to do the right thing, above all to use good judgment, but now good judgment felt as slippery as a trout in hand. By abandoning it, the kids had cut themselves loose. They were free agents in the cosmos. What did good judgment have to do with anything?

From where I stood just above the cushion of fog, I could see the lookout tower on Mount Fremont, also above the fog, glowing with a warm yellow light. I pictured Elise stationed at the radio, relaying flawless messages from Jack to Paradise on the west side of the mountain. I didn't plan to do what I did next.

Shivering, I headed back down Burrough's Mountain, cold and tired and hungry, thinking I would go home to bed. Instead, when I got to the junction at Frozen Lake, I started up Mount Fremont. As I approached I could see Elise's silhouette in the all-glass room at the top of her tower. Though I was still a quarter of a mile away, she came out on the tiny balcony that surrounded her glass perch. They were right when they said she missed nothing from her tower. I didn't call out or wave. So what if she was frightened by the approach of someone in the dead of night. That's what she got for being unfriendly at the cookout.

When I got to the base of the tower neither of us had spoken yet. I was disappointed to realize that Elise wasn't one bit scared. She looked annoyed. Her face said, "You?" I climbed the stairs and met her on the balcony. She wore a red and gray flannel shirt over a white T-shirt and Levi's.

"Did Jack send you?" Elise asked gruffly. She clearly didn't relish my intrusion.

"No. I was just out for a walk and landed here. Can I come in?" I was surprised at how aggressive I was being. For a femme out of uniform anyway.

She turned and entered her tiny room, leaving the door open. After I followed she went back to shut the door, filled a beat-up tin pan with water from a metal tank on the floor, and put the pan on a propane burner.

"I won't bother you. I mean, I know you're relaying messages for Jack."

"They won't need me anymore," she said, fingering the radio. "The eastside search-and-rescue team just made the top of the Inter Glacier. The westside party, going up from Paradise, just left with six climbers. Apparently the kids had talked about maybe going down the westside route and hitching back to White River."

Jack's voice came across the radio. It was fuzzy and distant, but I could pick up some of the words. "Bob, I want you to personally check the carabiners on each . . . Then we'll . . ." His voice faded out again.

Besides the radio, her tower was equipped with a map table, a direction finder and high-powered binoculars. Jack's voice faded in and out as I looked over her instruments and maps. "Where'd you learn to use all this stuff?" I asked.

She stopped to listen to Jack and didn't answer me.

"Jack knows exactly what he's doing," she finally said. "There's never a spare word in his communication. It's always tight and to the point."

So this was a mutual admiration party of two. She spoke of Jack with so much veneration I began to wonder if I'd been wrong about her being a lesbian. Maybe she was one of those types that was nothing, neither straight nor lesbian. She felt lesbian to me though. She definitely had dyke essence.

"Listen to him," Elise said, sitting down. She stirred instant-coffee crystals into two tin mugs. "He's perfect."

"That's a strong statement," I said, thinking about Jack's

auburn-haired wife, the fire in her eyes. The way she stood next to perfect Jack, her fingers curled around his biceps.

Elise nodded absently, agreeing. "Want chocolate in your coffee?"

"Sure."

"Are you hungry?"

I was very hungry and nodded.

Elise smiled at last. I felt as if I'd seen an endangered species.

As she opened a plastic bag of mixed dried fruit and put it on the map table, I stripped off my Gortex and down jacket. I was still shivering but wanted to be at home here in her glass room. She put on another pot of water and said, "I'll make soup."

In response to my questions, Elise showed me how the direction finder worked. She pointed out where the biggest fires of her tenure had occurred and explained exactly how she'd spotted them and what techniques had been used to smother them. Until she hurt her back she'd been a smoke jumper for the forest service, a fire fighter who jumped from helicopters into burns too deep in the wilderness to be reached by foot or road vehicle. Then she told me about the black bear she'd known since it was a cub that visited her several times a summer.

"She has a brown spot on the right side of her nose. Right here." Elise touched the place where her nose met her cheek. "Her paws are real pigeon-toed. All black bears are pigeon-toed, but she's more so."

Elise ran her hand down the side of her face and rested it on her neck. She looked soft, worn. "Anyway," she said, "she hadn't shown up this summer. I've been kind of, well, not exactly worried. She knows what's she's doing. She's a bear, after all. I just wondered where she was.

"Then yesterday," Elise stopped and cleared her throat of what sounded like welling tears. "Yesterday she brought her own cubs for me to see. Twins."

Elise walked over to the window, her back to me. She looked out at the night, shaking her head softly as if that sow and her cubs were all she needed in life. I envied Elise her containment. This tiny living space, her bears, her little propane burner.

"Have you named the bears?" I asked.

She turned quickly. "Of course not. They're bears. Not people."

"Do you feed them?"

"It's cruel to teach bears to rely on people."

I knew that of course. I spent half my days keeping park visitors from feeding chipmunks. But it wasn't common for bears to befriend people without a food motive. I had the feeling Elise thought it was cruel to teach *people* to rely on people. "So why you?" I asked. "Why did the bear choose you?"

"That's the million dollar question," she said without a trace of a smile. "Why me?"

Elise seemed a bit like a bear to me. She had that round, solid build and bright eyes. She embraced her strength rather than strutting it. She also had a clean, direct way of talking that moved her stories straight to my heart. I hadn't expected her to be a talker, especially not to a middle-of-the-night intruder. But she seemed blasé about my unexpected arrival, as if she had visitors on many nights. After we'd drunk two cups of mocha each, she ladled chicken noodle soup into my cup, without rinsing it, and set a box of crackers next to me. The way she offered food, holding it out in her hands as if they were paws, was both clumsy and tender. She had a way of approaching me—with the mug of soup, with the cracker box—then turning away quickly as if face to face was too intimate. She made me feel shy about looking her in the eye. We didn't talk as we dunked crackers into the soup and slurped up the noodles.

From the tower all I could see was the black night, and yet the light shifted minute by minute as the clouds moved, thinned and then thickened again. The hot drinks and our warm bodies heated the room and soon I was toasty.

"If you have to pee," she said, breaking the silence, "the outhouse is down the stairs and to the left."

I did. Outside I felt something stir in the night and turned, half-expecting the bear and her cubs, but it was something bigger—it was the wilderness itself stirring in my gut. When I returned Elise was sitting on her cot where she'd been when I left. Her back was against one of the glass windows and her legs laid open, one along the side of the cot and the other hanging off the edge. Instead of sitting back down on the stool by the map table, I sat on the cot and leaned back against her leg. Neither of us spoke for a long time. I let my body sink more deeply into the cot, against her leg, settling so that I was more *between* her legs. She picked up the foot that was on the floor and moved her legs so that they loosely encircled me. Outside, the forest of green-black trees extended for hundreds of miles in one direction. In the other, Mount Rainier rumbled gently in the night, three kids lost in the clouds blanketing her flanks, hot molten lava gurgling in her heart. Again, I felt the wilderness seize me, as if she were a lover.

I asked, "Do you know where the bear and her cubs live? I mean, do they have a den that you know of?"

Just then Jack's voice came, suddenly clear, on the radio. "Camp Sherman, come in."

Another man's voice, small and tinny but still audible, replied, "Roger."

Jack again, "Have you looked over the western ridge of Steamboat Prow? Over."

"Negative. But we have to turn back, Jack. It's starting to snow again. Hard. I can't risk the lives of the whole crew. Seeking permission to turn back. Over."

There was a long silence before Jack answered. Then, firmly, "Granted. Over."

"Ten-four. We'll stay at Camp Sherman tonight and try again in the . . ."

The voices faded again.

"The kids haven't a chance," I whispered. "Not overnight."

"Maybe," Elise answered. "Sounds like the searchers are going to camp at eleven thousand feet and try again in the morning. People have survived nights on the mountain. Maybe it'll clear."

"Maybe," I agreed.

A fresh onslaught of slushy rain began splatting against the windows. Elise reached up and pushed her fingers through my hair, starting at my neck and moving to the crown of my head. "I like curly hair," she said.

"Oh," I answered, surprised to hear her say something personal. She placed her other hand on my knee and pulled so that my legs were open. Then she traced the inseam of my jeans with her middle finger, moving from my knee up. "Your jeans are almost worn out," she said. Her hands were beautiful. They were strong and rough, the fingernails bitten.

I wished I could have answered with something just as casual, but I didn't trust my voice. The wind whistled across the roof of her tower. The windows shook. She scooted forward so that she was pressed against my hip and then she tightened the grip of her legs around me. I didn't even know this woman but she turned my body to absolute desire. And though I was the one who'd placed myself between her legs, I fought it.

"The bears . . ." I started again. "Their den . . . Do you know?"

Her fingers moved gracefully as she undid the buttons of my shirt and pulled it off my shoulders. I sat on the cot in my worn jeans and bra while she slipped onto her knees on the floor and unbuttoned my pants. I realized then that she wasn't even going to take off her boots. Oh, who was this woman?

I felt myself giving in to something dangerous, as if I were about to enter the mountain blizzard as foolishly willing as those three kids. I held myself back. I said, "I didn't come here for this." Elise didn't answer. Her strong hands tugged my jeans down over my hips. The voices on the radio scratched on and off as the steam on the windows of the glass walls sealed us in. I began to disappear into the hollow of my belly, somewhere much deeper than my own body.

Elise pushed me back on the cot and leaned down to take a nipple, through my bra, into her mouth. Her hands cradled my neck for a while, as if this were going to be very tender lovemaking, but soon she slid them across my collarbone, briefly gripping my shoulders, and then moving down my sides and over my hips. She handled me roughly now, as if she were desperate for the nourishment my breasts, belly and thighs gave her. I struggled to stay in my body, but I could no more return from this journey than those kids could find their way down the mountain this stormy night. As I came the first time, my mind slipped away, disappeared altogether, and I found myself in a foreign land. It was like the universe, black with stars all around. It was like the top of the mountain, desolate and empty, yet all I could ever need. It was a land that predated all that I knew to be true. As if creation were happening all around me. In and through me.

Some time later—I didn't know whether seconds or hours had passed—I returned to the lookout tower. Elise was rocking between my legs, her fist still in me. My head hung so far off her cot it nearly touched the floor, but she had one arm securely behind my shoulders to keep it from bonking on the wooden planks. Seeing I had come back, she effortlessly lifted my head and shoulders onto the cot. I know I looked at her with uncompromised worship. "Don't," was all she said. And I knew she was right. It wasn't Elise, it was that land on the other side that had made me reverent.

We dozed together on her cot, and when I awoke the sky had lightened. The tiny room smelled musky and hot. The back of my throat ached with desire, an aftertaste I knew would never go away. Elise got up and cracked open the door to clear the steamy windows. The clouds had fled and a scattering of stars still remained in the paling sky. I lay on the cot, not moving, and watched the mountain turn peach and then bright yellow as the sun rose. The storm had lifted. Could the kids still be alive? I loved Elise for not saying, "You'd better go," though she was already at her instruments, measuring wind speed and direction, reading her barometer, recording the morning's temperature, writing down the exact moment of sunrise.

Messages were singing across her radio. She seemed to ignore them until suddenly she pivoted and took up the radio. A voice was calling urgently, "Fremont, come in. Fremont, come in."

"This is Fremont. Go ahead." Elise was all business.

"We found 'em. One mile from Paradise." The voice paused. For a moment, I thought he meant the bears. I heard a sharp exhale of breath. Then, "All three dead. Transmit to Jack and stand by. Over."

"Ten-four. Verify message for Jack: Three climbers found dead one mile from Paradise. Over."

"Ten-four. Over and out."

"Over and out."

Elise didn't even look at me. She called Jack. "Communication from the Paradise search-and-rescue: The three climbers were found dead one mile from Paradise. Over."

Jack was silent for a long time. "Shit," he said into the radio. Jack, who usually followed radio protocol to the letter, yelled, "Shit,

shit, *shit.*"

Elise waited. Then she spoke, "Jack, is there anything you want to relay? Over."

"Negative. Stand by. Over and out."

"Ten-four. Over and out."

I dressed quickly, then walked over and put a hand on Elise's shoulder. "I'm going now," I said. My hand was shaking.

"Okay, then." Elise stood up and put her hands in her front pockets. She looked me dead in the eye, as she had with Jack at the cookout. I felt inadequate in the face of that look. I knew my own eyes swam with sleeplessness and utter fulfillment, that my hair was foolishly smashed to one side.

"The kids," I said. I wanted to cry so badly.

Elise nodded.

They had only wanted to climb the mountain. They came all the way from Wisconsin. I left, running down the wooden stairs of her tower, crying hard as I jogged the five miles to my cabin at Sunrise. I was fifteen minutes late opening the Visitor Center.

I couldn't think of anything but the three dead teenagers. And Elise. Night after night I kept myself from stalking back out to her lookout tower. I tried to use up my energy by running out to the end of Sourdough Ridge and roaming through the Silver Forest. One night I even swam at midnight in Sunrise Lake, stroking through the black and icy glacial water. The lake was deep, and at the bottom lay a thick mud where all kinds of slimy worms and crustacea lived. I flipped over on my back and floated, touching myself and thinking of Elise. Everything had become unbearably immediate. I ached with the loss of the young climbers. I longed to have back that afternoon at the Emmons Glacier lookout so I could memorize their faces, talk with them more, learn of their climbing plans, even convince them not to climb. Ironically, though, I still loved them for climbing in spite of the weather, and I didn't care that my obsession with them was almost perverse. Not when I threw Elise into the mix. The night of lovemaking and the death of the kids all fused inside me.

And the relief! At last, my longing for Donna, as well as my visions of homicide, began to fade. I even found myself feeling grateful that Donna had left me so that I could be here for this.

Yet I knew better than to take anything from Elise for granted. I had felt, even in the heat of that night in her tower, something in Elise that was like a pause. Not uncertainty—the way she made love was more certain than anything I'd ever felt—but a skipped beat, a delay. I knew I could overcome it with my steady, full-on loving, but I'd have to be careful, go easy. Oh, I knew Elise didn't want me charging after her, but I could make her come for me. And I would. I swore every waking moment that I would.

Once a week I gave an evening campfire program down at the White River campground. A couple of weeks after the kids died I asked Jack Keeney to be a guest speaker at the campfire program. I told him that with all the media hype about The Fatalities—the term everyone now used, which on one hand upset me in its cold finality, and on the other hand comforted me in its distant formality—the public might like to hear some factual information about how climbing is controlled on the mountain and how search-and-rescue operations work. What I really wanted was to know Jack Keeney better, to find out what composed Elise's idea of "perfect."

"Good idea," he agreed. "Meet in the parking lot at six. We'll take my truck."

I arrived five minutes early and was waiting by the Park Service truck when he emerged from the backcountry office. He nodded his head toward the far side of the parking lot. "*My* truck," he said, meaning his personal truck, a new blue Jimmy.

He surprised me by actually being able to make small talk as we drove the nine miles down to the campground. In the off-season he taught math and chemistry at a community college. His wife Barbara had a small design company. She was hired by stores and organizations to design exhibits and brochures. He drove with one arm cocked behind him, the elbow resting on the truck seat, the other hand on top of the steering wheel. I got the feeling he had no doubts whatsoever about what was right and what was wrong. Not a trace of ambiguity.

"How many seasons have you been working on the mountain?" I asked.

"Twelve."

"Just two more than Elise."

"That's right."

"There ought to be a party or something," I said. "You know, to celebrate Elise being at the Mount Fremont lookout for ten years."

He gave me a funny look. Then smiled a little. I liked his dimples. I smiled back. "You know Elise?" he asked.

"Oh, not really." The thought of her hands made me weak. If he or I said her name one more time I'd slide off the seat to the truck floor like something viscous.

Jack laughed, said, "Elise," and shook his head.

Something hard in his voice, the way he encapsulated her name, made me freeze up rather than slide. He gave her name a hollow sound and I glimpsed a crack in Jack's composure. A quick slump in his posture. A swallowing look in his eyes. He took his elbow off the seat and gripped the steering wheel with both hands, at ten o'clock and two o'clock.

Maybe I was reading way too much into Jack. He was Elise's symbol of perfection, so he'd become a text for me, too meaningful. He was just Jack Keeney, back country ranger extraordinaire. Big deal.

The campfire talk went well. Jack rarely related directly to the public, his job being behind the scenes, but he was good at it. They loved his hard truths, his obvious devotion to saving lives at whatever cost, the pain he was willing to show about the deaths of those kids. "Useless," he said. "Absolutely unnecessary." I liked the way he talked about them because although he referred—rightly—to the kids' stupidity in climbing when they shouldn't have, he left room for their humanity. I felt that he'd agree with me that death wasn't a fair punishment for ignoring storm warnings.

Afterwards, when we'd climbed back in his truck, I told him what the skinny boy had said to me that day at the Emmons Glacier viewpoint.

Jack nodded, like he understood but wouldn't allow any excess sentimentality. "Let's get a drink," he said.

I was startled. I wanted to say, "Why?" but what came out was, "Where?"

"There's a bar just down the hill a few miles."

We rode in silence. After awhile, he turned off the highway and down a wide dirt road. I wondered briefly about my safety, then reminded myself that Jack was a legend, had been on the mountain for twelve years. If he was a womanizer, I would have heard. I think. He pulled the Jimmy in front of a backwoods tavern, made of whole logs, with smoke puffing out of a stone chimney. I leapt down from the truck and followed him in the door. They knew him. The bartender poured a double Scotch and looked at me. "The same," I said, nodding at Jack's drink. I worried for a second about drinking in our uniforms, but I was with Jack.

We took a table near the fireplace. Jack settled back and drank, slowly and with concentration. Not like an alcoholic but like a man who wanted to feel his Scotch. I realized this night had nothing to do with me. He wanted the drink and I just happened to have been in the truck with him. I appreciated the silence, it actually felt rather companionable. I looked up at the moose head directly above me. A bear's head jutted out over the bar. I wondered if Jack knew about Elise's bear. I wondered how I could get him to talk about her.

He put down his empty glass and said, "So, you married? Have a boyfriend?"

"I had a girlfriend until recently," I told him, wondering whatever made me think I could come out to Jack, of all people. Still I blazed on, "She left me for someone else."

The bartender arrived with the bottle of Scotch and poured us two more doubles.

"Ain't that a bitch," Jack said. At first I thought he was cussing at my lesbianism, but then I decided he was sympathizing with my being dumped.

"Yeah," I said.

"You'll find someone new. Elise is a lesbian. Is that why you were asking me questions about her?"

"Uh," I said. I couldn't keep up with this man. "No, uh."

Jack leaned across the table and said, "Know what I'd do to someone who touched my wife?"

I shook my head, wishing I'd never ventured into this subject. "I wouldn't touch your wife, Jack," I said vehemently. "I'm not interested in straight women and even if I was—"

Jack cracked up laughing and reached across the table and took my hand. "No, no, no," he said, the Scotch softening his gestures. "I didn't mean that. I'm not worried about you touching Barbara. I only meant to tell you how I'd feel, what I'd do, if someone did to me what that woman did to you. Now, do you know what I'd do to someone who touched my wife?"

I really didn't. Jack felt like a black hole to me right then. I felt sucked into his swirl of intensity and unexpected warmth.

"What?" I said. "What would you do?"

He sat back in his chair and rested an ankle on one knee. He laughed, beckoned the bartender. "I'm not worried about competition," he said. "It's not an issue for me."

Looking at Jack it was hard not to picture him having sex. It wasn't a perverse thought. It was just that he had such hard energy, so oddly moralistic and vibrant at once. I wondered if it had something to do with his military experience and found myself asking, "So how long were you in Vietnam?"

For a moment I thought he'd hit me. You'd think I'd said, "I heard your mother eats dog shit" or "Barbara tells me your penis is pencil-thin." Leave it to me to step on the one spot you weren't supposed to step on. Something about Jack made everything move too fast.

"I'm sorry," I said forcefully. "Forget I asked that. Let's talk some more about what I should do to my girlfriend. How I should handle being treated so badly. Tell me what you'd do to anyone caught touching—"

"I told you that wasn't my issue," he repeated but he laughed again now. "I like you. Come on. Let's go." We both threw back the last of our third double Scotches.

I almost needed help getting into the Jimmy this time. The first step was about two feet high and I was pretty drunk. Jack climbed in the driver's side and waited for me to claw my way up. So much for my trying to prove to him I was a good climber. I couldn't even get up into a large truck.

He didn't start the engine, just sat there. I waited, way over on my side of the seat. Finally, as if he'd decided something, he turned the ignition. Then he drove slowly back up the road.

"Why'd you think I might be interested in Elise?" I asked.

He put his elbow back on the seat, draped his hand over the top of the steering wheel again. "I don't know if you would or not, but there's not a lot of choice up here, is there? If you're a lesbian, I mean."

I laughed. "I guess I can go without for a summer."

"But why would you?"

I felt uncomfortable again. I glanced at him and he was looking at me with that intent boy look. Then he reached out and slapped the side of my leg with the back of his hand. "Just kidding, Tracy. Relax."

"I hate it when men tell me to relax."

He nodded. "Okay," he said. "Sorry."

At Sunrise Point, just three miles below Sunrise where the road does a big hairpin turn, Jack pulled over. He got out and slammed the door. I waited in the car, thinking maybe he was going to pee. He jumped over the short stone wall and disappeared down into the brush. I was right. When he reappeared, he was zipping up his fly. He opened the truck door again, reached into the cab behind the seat, and took out a rifle. "Get out," he said.

"Jesus," I whispered. He stood in front of the truck beckoning me with the hand that wasn't holding the rifle. His Park Service uniform was a mess, the sleeves rolled up unevenly, the shirttails hanging out of the pants. His crew cut looked cruel, like a million needles sticking out of his head. Now he headed around to my door and as I reached to jam down the lock, he yanked it open.

"Come on," he said. "I want to show you something." Then he saw the fear in my eyes. He stopped, leaned the gun against the truck. "Tracy," he said. "For god's sake. Are all lesbians as frightened of men as you? What do you think I'm gonna do?"

Then I felt like a fool. There I was in my Class As, complete with brass buttons and badge, worrying about rape. Not that it couldn't happen, but who rapes Smokey the Bear?

"You take the gun," Jack said, motioning impatiently at it.

So I finally jumped out of the truck and took the gun.

"Ever shot one before?"

"No."

Jack stood behind me, the way boys do when they are teaching you how to swing a baseball bat, and positioned the rifle on my shoulder and in my hands. Then he turned my whole body around and told me, "Find that Slow sign in the viewer." I did. "Now squeeze the trigger."

I lowered the rifle and turned to look at Jack.

"It's fun," he said. "Just do it." He grinned, his dimples taking up half his face. "Give it to me. Watch."

Jack aimed the rifle and shot at the metal sign. The sound it made, a combination of ping and explosion, was terribly satisfying. A clean black hole pierced the yellow sign. I started over to examine it, but Jack yelled, "Stay back, damnit." When I returned to his side, he plugged three more holes in the sign. Then he gave the rifle back to me. Again, he stood behind me and positioned everything just right. He stepped back. I pulled the trigger. Something slammed against my jaw so hard I nearly dropped the gun.

"Whoa, whoa," Jack said, taking it from me as gently as if it were a baby. "Easy now. She has a little bit of a kick, don't she?"

I touched my jaw where the butt of the rifle had struck, feeling thrilled and exhausted.

"I should have warned you." Jack walked the gun back to the truck and put it behind the seat again. Then he came and sat by me on the stone ledge. He said, "Tomorrow I'll call the Highway Department. Order a new one."

I looked at him, trying to decide if he felt any regret for ruining the Slow sign. He met my eyes and smiled. "Tracy," he said, touching my hand lightly. "I'd like to sleep with you."

"Oh come on," I said, rolling my eyes. "Give me a break!" The strange thing was that I was almost tempted. Maybe it was the Scotch, but I took his hand and wove my fingers through his. I knew Elise loved him, at least revered him, and I wanted to feel what she knew. But I said, "No." Then I said it again. "No."

"I don't care if you're a lesbian," he said. "That doesn't matter to me."

I laughed at his self-centeredness. "But it matters to me. *I* care that I'm a lesbian."

"What, being a lesbian means you can never have dick?"

"No. I just don't ***want***, uh, dick."

"Well, I can understand that. Neither do I." He looked me in the eye again and we laughed.

I reached up and touched his jaw, amazed as I always am by the scratchiness of a man's face.

"Besides," I said. "What about what you'd do to someone who touched your wife? Doesn't that cut both ways?"

"Cut," he said. "I like that word. Yeah, it cuts both ways. *She* definitely does." He jumped off the stone wall. "Let's go."

A couple minutes later, when I came into my cabin at midnight, Beth put down her book and sighed. It was two hours past her bedtime. "Oh, Tracy," she said. "I was quite worried about you."

"I'm sorry," I said. She hardly knew me, yet apparently I was all she had to worry about. "I'm really sorry," I repeated, and went to bed.

I lay there until four in the morning trying to understand Elise, Jack, and their relationship. I went over and over my conversations with both of them, looking for intersections. I found none.

◆ ◆ ◆

I called Donna that week, feeling confident I was ready for the next phase—a short phone conversation. Besides, I wanted to talk to someone familiar, someone without a shred of mystery attached to her. I also wanted to tell her about The Fatalities. There was no one else I could talk to about those deaths, how I couldn't get the picture of them out of my head. Sometimes I saw them tangled all three together, the skinny boy finally being included in the embrace of the other two, their eyes frozen open, blank. Other times I imagined them separated, some final blowout causing them to split up on the climb, the emotional tension among them being the cause of their deaths. The more I thought of the kids, the more I needed to touch Elise, relive that night in her tower. Maybe I also wanted Donna to know I'd been loved, if only for a night, though of course I wouldn't tell her that. She'd know though. She'd hear it in my voice. I'd make her hear it.

An unfamiliar voice answered Donna's phone, a hesitant, pale voice. Lurking Dog. Answering Donna's telephone! I had a full-body flashback to firing that rifle. I wanted to feel it slam against my jaw, hear that pow-ping sound as I exploded holes in the sign that said Slow. A million ugly words crowded my throat and I hung up before I said any of them.

Then I felt ashamed. It'd be one thing if I was an alcoholic, or maybe if I had a background of abuse, but there was no explanation for my ugliness, beyond raging jealousy. I thought being with Elise, at least my obsession with her, had loosened my grip on that jealousy, but the sound of Lurking Dog's voice made me realize how far I had yet to go.

But how would I go that distance? Elise seemed like the whole answer to me, everything I wanted, though I knew so little about her. That place she'd shown me, that other side, I thought only she could lead me there again. And yet, as badly as I wanted her, somehow I knew that to return to Elise would be to miss the point. The coordinates of time and space had brought us together for a moment, and it was this coincidence that made it work for her, maybe even for me. She certainly hadn't sought me out since that night. I should let our moment together explode like a star, hot and bright, a thing unto itself. Yet I couldn't. I wanted to be touched by her calloused hands again. I wanted to see her dark brown eyes that looked like soil, like hard work. I wanted to touch her strong back and feel her skilled strength deliver me outside of myself.

So I planned a business trip to see her. Part of my job, after all, was patrolling the trails. On a Saturday in August, I put on my Class Bs, the informal uniform I was supposed to wear in the field, and hiked out to Mount Fremont, preparing to spend the busy afternoon rangering. It was a popular hike. It made perfect sense that I'd station myself there for a few hours and interpret the sights for the visitors.

The afternoon was vibrant with color, the mountain glossy white like a huge meringue against the sapphire sky. The lupine and paintbrush ached with purple and red. I had the sense of passion swirling all around me but not touching me.

There wasn't a visitor in sight as I approached the tower. Elise came out on the balcony, waved, then clumped down the stairs as if she were happy to see me. Had I been all wrong? Maybe she'd been waiting for me, too shy to approach!

"I was going to call you on the radio," she said.

"You were?"

"But I knew I shouldn't. Not about this."

I waited, thinking *at last.*

She said, "Remember you asked about where the bears live? I think I've found their den."

What's this got to do with us, I wondered, but asked, "Where?"

She pointed down the valley, well beyond Berkeley Park, to a ridge. "See that isolated stand of pines? Just up the hill from it. There's a small rock outcropping with a cave."

"Have you been searching?"

"Sort of. It's something to do with my time off."

I didn't point out that most people use their days off to go into town to do laundry and buy supplies.

"I've been wanting to talk with you," I said, emboldened by her enthusiasm. "The way you live on this mountaintop, in this glass tower, it makes it a little difficult to be subtle. Either I've come to see you or I haven't."

"We're both on the job now," she said, withdrawing her warmth so fast I felt a breeze. She looked off down the valley, toward the ridge where the bears lived, as if she'd sooner lie down with them before she would with me again.

"I, uh, don't understand why, when you come into Sunrise, you don't, you know, at least stop in the VC or my cabin to say hi. I mean, after that night we had together."

Elise gnawed on her baby fingernail. "I've only been down to Sunrise a couple of times."

"I know. And both times I watched you walk right by the VC without even looking inside." I reached out and touched her cheek with the back of my hand. I was surprised she didn't jerk back. Instead she took my hand and kissed my knuckles. She didn't look at me as she shook her head and said, "You're beautiful, Tracy. I like everything about you."

I waited, but that was all. No throwing me onto the soil and ripping off my Class Bs right there, which I would have let her do, busy August Saturday afternoon or not. No invitations to come back tonight, when we weren't both on the job.

Was it the distance between our homes? If it was, I'd move to her town in Michigan the minute the season was over. I was there. I was packed. The word "bulldozer" flashed through my brain, along with Donna's accusations that I thought I could "fix" anything my way, fashion a life as if it were playdough. And why not?

The answer was somewhere in Elise's body language. She'd kissed my hand, but she was withdrawing.

Then she said, "Visitors."

I looked over my shoulder and here came a family of three. The man came right for me and before two minutes had passed I'd learned about the land in Idaho where they would move as soon as they got the cash together, the superiority of home-schooling, the centrality of Christ in their lives. As he filled me in on his family's life, his towheaded kid and young wife orbiting about his legs, Elise returned to her tower. I felt her departure like skin ripping off my body.

"Why not me?" I wanted to scream after her. Why the evasiveness? Was it about Jack? Was there some girlfriend to whom she was being faithful? If so, why didn't she just tell me?

"You know," I interrupted the man's monologue, "I know of no better way to get closer to god than to hike back down to the fork in the trail at Frozen Lake, and from there hike up to second Burrough's Mountain. If you don't have visions of his glory up there, then you're a poor wretched soul."

The man stared at me. At least I'd shut him up. I guess he decided I'd been sincere because he said, "Well, thank you, uh, Sister—" He was apparently far-sighted because he had to lean in and practically put his face on my breast to read my name tag. "Sister Tracy. We'll do that." At least he hadn't called me "rangerette" like half of them do. He picked up the kid and off they went.

The thing was, I wasn't being facetious about second Burrough's mountain and god's glory. I meant it.

I looked up at the tower and saw Elise on the radio. I'd feel like a fool just hanging around out here on top of Mount Fremont, as if I was waiting for time with her, which was what I would be doing. She knew exactly why I'd come and she'd said what she had to say. So I waved up at her, she waved back, and I hiked slowly, to avoid the home-schooling Christian family, back to Frozen Lake. There I stood looking at the mountain for a long time. It was so glorious today, I thought it a shame the kids had been found. I'd rather be buried in one of the glaciers than in some grassy cemetery plot in Wisconsin. Not wanting to return to the Visitor Center, I started walking up the Burrough's Mountain trail, straight toward the mountain.

Occasionally a red Miata would pull into the parking area and my heart would lurch. Once one arrived with the top down and two women sitting in the bucket seats, the driver tall and blond. A mix of joy and anger catapulted me toward the parking lot, but as I approached the Visitor Center exit, I knocked over the book rack by the door. Hundreds of dollars worth of nature books crashed to the floor, their covers bending and corners crushing. By the time I picked them all up and arranged them back on the rack, the two women from the Miata were coming in the Visitor Center door. The tall blonde looked nothing like Donna.

Still, the adrenaline surged through my system all afternoon and evening, like a triple espresso, making me feel crazy and definitely preventing sleep. So late that night, I tracked back out to Elise's fire tower, moving like a shadow. My plan was to stop at a distance and only watch her. If I was lucky she'd be up with her lantern lit.

As I approached I saw that her lantern was indeed lit. I scuttled along the trail, keeping my eyes lowered so I wouldn't attract her attention, and ducked behind a large boulder about fifty yards from the tower. I was breathing hard and afraid she'd already detected my presence. Slowly I eased my head around the side of the boulder to look.

There was someone in the tower with Elise. Two women were silhouetted against the night. One woman had her hands braced behind her on what would be Elise's map table, her head thrown back. My view gave me a perfect profile and I could see the woman's open mouth and her hair hanging freely behind her head. Her breasts lifted up to the ceiling of the tower. Another head was between her legs.

"Sweet Jesus," I murmured, sinking back behind the boulder.

I shifted my weight and an old piece of wood cracked, sounding like an explosion in the stillness of the night. I froze. I counted to ten. Then I slid my head around the rock again to see if I'd caught their attention. Hardly. Elise's head was still decidedly between the woman's legs. She stayed like that for what seemed like hours, the other woman's mouth opening and closing in what appeared to be gasps, her hips rocking back and forth in Elise's hands.

I watched. I wanted that to be me. I wondered why it wasn't. I ran my hands down my breasts, across my thighs. I leaned back against my boulder and moaned. I remembered every tiny nuance of my own night in that tower.

Finally the woman pulled Elise up by her collar and they sunk into a long kiss, the woman lying back on the map table now and Elise pressing on top of her. After awhile the stranger pushed Elise off and reached for something on the floor. Her shirt. Elise helped her get her arms in it and then tenderly buttoned it up for her. With me Elise hadn't been so much tender as she'd been deft. Even at this distance I could see that Elise became malleable in the presence of this other woman.

The woman moved quickly now, as if she were late. She pulled on her jacket, kissed Elise again, and hurried out of the glass room and down the stairs of the tower. Shit! I hadn't thought about being discovered by the stranger! There was no way I could escape without being seen. I had to wait behind the boulder and pray she would not see me as she passed on the trail just three yards away. I watched the woman approach. She hadn't come very far along the trail when I recognized Jack Keeney's wife, Barbara.

I literally collapsed. I hugged the earth as if it were the only sure thing in existence. Jack Keeney's wife!

I forced myself to get up. There'd be time for shock later. I had to get well out of sight. I pressed up against the back of the boulder, held my breath, and watched her half-run past me on the trail. She looked beautiful, her hair bright in the moonlight, her gait loose and easy. When she was out of sight I looked back at the tower.

I couldn't believe what I'd seen. Everything I'd heard about Jack and Barbara's marriage.... The part that confused me the most was the way Elise nearly worshipped Jack. Her boss. She hadn't faked her esteem for him—why would she? It was as real as those bullet holes through the Slow sign.

I couldn't help myself. I waited a respectable amount of time and then stepped out from behind my rock and headed up to the fire tower. As I drew close, I saw Elise blow out her lantern.

I started up the stairs. My footsteps echoing on the lumber startled her. She called out, "Barbara?" She thought her lover had returned.

She had, but not the one she expected.

"Barbara!" This time her voice was urgent.

I paused a moment. Then I called out, "It's me."

Elise appeared at her door in a full suit of red long underwear. She looked softer than I'd ever seen her. I wanted to touch her, but a vulnerable butch is something you don't mess with, so I stopped my approach, like an animal who understands territory.

She was literally speechless.

I said, "I saw everything." Trying to lighten the mood, I added, "So how many women traipse out here for your services, anyway? I thought your job was putting out fires."

Elise looked me over good and long, still speechless and maybe frightened. She knew next to nothing about me, and I had first-class blackmail information on her.

"Can I come in?" I asked.

She stepped out of the doorway and let me in.

Elise had been crying. I noticed the wet patch on her pillow, the red blotches on her face, her eyelashes clumped together with tears. I stood awkwardly next to the map table, not knowing what to do but unwilling to leave.

She suddenly began sobbing. "I don't cry," she forced out between sobs. "I don't cry in front of people."

"You are now," I said softly, deciding I'd better not try holding her. "You are now."

I filled her tin pan with water from the tank. Then I fiddled around trying to light her propane burner, which provided her with the opportunity to get up, push me aside and do it herself. That helped. She paced for a while, looking more like a bear than ever.

"Ten years this year," she began, wiping her nose on her sleeve. "Barbara and I have been lovers for ten years, ever since my first summer up here." She laughed hoarsely and ran her hands through her short hair. "Oh, we've broken it off a million times, sometimes me and sometimes her. One summer we made it through the whole season without having sex once."

"Why doesn't she leave Jack?"

Elise looked at me as if I were crazy. "Jack doesn't have anything to do with it."

It seemed to me that Jack would have everything to do with it.

"Does he know?" I asked, going through our conversations in my mind, trying to decide if I'd detected knowledge.

"Of course not. They have a perfect relationship. Jack . . . Jack, he's . . . ." For a moment Elise seemed at a loss for words. Then, "Jack is so solid. No woman in her right mind would ever leave Jack. You know, he was a POW in Vietnam. He's the kind of person that every year you know him you learn more. I love Barbara too much to ever want her to leave Jack. Ever." Elise was almost growling now.

I forced myself to keep quiet, but oh how I wanted to clear up her misconceptions about flawless Jack.

After a long silence, she whispered huskily, "But . . ."

I waited.

"But every time she leaves me it's harder. Every single year it gets wilder, bigger, deeper." She turned off the boiling water and scrounged around for a tea bag. "I spend every winter ravaging women at home in Michigan, looking for one who can call up the passion Barbara calls up in me. But Barbara, she's this rock in my heart." Elise was fierce. "Do you understand?"

I nodded. I thought I did. I wondered how many of those ravaged women in Michigan felt as awed by Elise as I did now.

"You're the only person I've ever told."

I was amazed by her ability to hold such an enormous secret, but I believed that she had. "I swear I won't ever tell anyone."

Elise smiled softly, nodded a little. I certainly meant it and I think she believed me.

I waited for her to say something more, but she was quiet. She made only one cup of peppermint tea. I could tell she wanted to be alone. I was no replacement for Barbara. I stood to go.

For a long moment I watched Elise stirring sugar into her tea. I wished I'd never had that evening with Jack. I wished I didn't know everything I knew. I wished I knew a lot more than I knew.

She didn't look up from her tin cup of tea as I stepped out of her glass room and shut the door behind me. The last I saw of Elise, through the window before I went down the stairs, she was sitting on her cot, in the same position she'd been in the time I'd sat between her legs.

Most Park Service employees left the mountain right after Labor Day weekend. I was asked to stay on a couple more weeks, until the snow closed the road for the year, and I reluctantly agreed. I didn't much want to stay, but I didn't want to go home either. Donna expected me back in town the day after Labor Day. I enjoyed thinking about how I just wouldn't show up. I was sure she'd call my apartment, that three months of being totally out of touch would be more than even she could bear, but I wouldn't be there. She wouldn't be able to find me.

Both the number of park visitors and the temperature dropped radically after Labor Day. I tried to make the most of the situation. Beth had left and I loved having the cabin to myself. I loved the clarity of the autumn air. And I liked the park visitors who came in September. They were more serious, true mountain devotees.

Elise was still out in the lookout tower, but at Sunrise, besides me and a scaled down maintenance staff, Barbara and Jack were the only ones left. They avoided me for the most part.

One September night I hiked out into the Silver Forest and sat down in the soil, my back against a weathered snag. The moon was a half-disc, polished and cold-looking, and I shivered at it, as if it were a giant ice cube cooling the air. I wondered what I'd do when I left the mountain in a couple of weeks. I felt ragged and unfinished, as if I'd begun a journey then forgotten where I was supposed to be going.

From where I sat in the Silver Forest, the trail disappeared around a corner a few feet away. Barbara appeared from around that bend, panting, like some kind of phantom.

I screamed. Which made her scream.

Most people would have laughed at the mutual scare, but I demanded, "What are you doing here?" wanting to ask if she haunted every corner of this mountain. Who took care of her in the Silver Forest like Elise did on Mount Fremont?

Barbara stared at me for a moment. Hostilely? I could hardly read her face even in the bright moonlight.

She breathed heavily, as if she'd been jogging up the trail, and didn't answer me. The whites of her eyes flashed moonlight briefly and she turned, disappearing back down the trail again, like a critter.

A week or so later, on the first day that the temperature never rose above freezing, I spent the morning running back and forth between the Visitor Center and my cabin, baking oatmeal cookies. I took a plate of hot ones over to Jack in the backcountry office and found Barbara there too, nestled in the rocker in front of the wood-burning stove, with a tattered paperback from the wood box. I almost wished I could curl up on the rug at their feet like their pet. They created such an enticing illusion of comfort.

Barbara never even smiled at me during those three weeks in September, though I felt her interest. It didn't feel like curiosity exactly, more like the kind of recognition animals give one another. I know you, her eyes said, though I felt confident Elise had told her nothing—Elise wouldn't—but Barbara knew I was a lesbian, her only competition on the mountain. At times I wanted to rub it in her face. I wanted her to feel that I was a real lesbian, not one hiding in a "perfect" heterosexual marriage. I'd put on an air of swaggering confidence, tried to look like a woman who was more than satisfied. Who, I wanted her to wonder, had satisfied me? As much as I studied Barbara, I could never understand what Elise found so irresistible. True, she was good-looking, a lot like Meryl Streep only without the excessive coyness and not so pointy, but she didn't light my fire.

As for Jack, he treated me as if we'd never had that evening together, except that he remembered my name. If he wasn't on the radio or too absorbed in paperwork when I came into the backcountry office, he'd nod at me, say, "How are ya?" That was all.

I was awed by the balance that they—Jack, Barbara, and Elise—had struck, this ten-year stasis. And yet, Elise was the one alone in the glass tower. Still. Waiting, I guessed, but for what?

Two weeks into September it began to snow. It snowed off and on for three days. Jack announced that the park would close after the weekend. I began packing, planning on leaving first thing Monday morning. On Saturday afternoon Jack came into the Visitor Center.

"You got a call last night. A woman named Donna. You weren't in your cabin." Jack leaned against the counter I stood behind and grinned at me, acknowledging for the first time in weeks that we knew each other a little better than casually.

"Did she leave a message?"

"She wanted to know if you were still on the mountain." Jack smiled wickedly. "I told her I didn't know where you were."

"Jack!" I said, partly delighted and partly worried. "You're evil."

"Some say so." He started to leave.

"Wait. What else did she say?"

"She sounded a little panicked. Wanted to know if you'd mentioned going anywhere when you left here."

"And?"

"I told her I had no information." He seemed to relish torturing Donna for me. I appreciated the loyalty, if that's what it was, but was a little frightened by his meanness. I told Jack thanks as he left.

I was touched Donna had tried to reach me, but I didn't call her that night. I did write to her, though, and, for the first time in months, found words useful. I wrote for hours. I told her about the deaths of the three kids, about Elise and me, about Jack and Barbara. I told her how I'd come to enjoy the immensity of the universe and my insignificance in it, how I'd learned the joy in being too small to make a difference.

The next night as I packed someone knocked on my door. Barbara Keeney let herself in before I even answered. She'd never once been in my room.

"Excuse me," she said. "Can I come in?"

"Sure. Sit down."

Barbara looked bruised, not physically, but in her facial posture, the way she held her mouth, her eyes. She didn't sit down. She twisted a strand of hair in her fingers and said, "I wondered if you've seen Elise lately."

I felt my face go hot. "No," I said, feeling as if I was lying, then realizing I wasn't. Two nights ago I'd slunk out there yet again. It was her last night on the job and I wasn't counting on her coming to say goodbye to me before she started the drive home to Michigan. I wanted one last look, so I waited behind the big boulder for her to reveal herself. I saw a small spotlight, probably from her flashlight, flick about the tower. I figured she was lying on her cot reading. I wanted her to get up and go out to pee so I could see her whole body. I wanted her to sit up suddenly and say to herself, *She's here, I can feel her.* Then she'd run down the wooden stairs in her bare feet straight to my hiding place. She'd hold out a hand and say, *Come, Tracy.* Of course that hadn't happened. So I had finally stood, stepped from behind my boulder, made my presence blatant, tried to send rays of energy to draw her. But in fact Elise was human, not a bear. She didn't have extraordinary powers of smell or any extra animal sense, not really. I could have intruded again, climbed up those stairs one last time, but somewhere deep inside me, I'd begun to learn that I wanted something she had more than I wanted her.

Finally the tiny spotlight blinked off. I pictured her curling up in her sleeping bag, probably thinking about Barbara's kiss, and I walked home slowly.

I said to Barbara, "Her car is right out there in the lot where it always is."

But of course Barbara knew that. "I know," she said. "That's just it. She was supposed to have come out yesterday, start for home today. She never came out. We can't get her on the radio."

"What does Jack say?"

"He says Elise knows what she's doing and she'll contact us when she gets back to the tower."

"Well, then."

"Jack treats Elise like a man."

"Meaning?"

"He respects her complete independence."

"Well, so do I."

Barbara said, "I don't." Tears filled her eyes.

Discomfort made me laugh. "You know Elise. She doesn't even come out for her days off. I bet she's just hanging out a little extra, has the radio off because she's off duty." I thought Barbara was overreacting.

"Last night," Barbara said. "I walked out there." She raised her chin a bit as if to say, don't you dare ask me why.

"And?"

"Elise wasn't there."

"At night?"

"No."

"Was her stuff there?"

"Yes."

"Maybe she wanted to do a bit of backcountry camping before—"

"Her sleeping bag, all her gear, was in the tower. Why won't anyone listen! Elise is gone. She's not there!" Barbara gulped air and went on, "And the tower looks like it's closed for the winter, everything's done except for the boards on the windows. She's gone, been gone for at least twenty-four hours, and her gear's there."

"Shit," I whispered. I thought of Elise's desperate tears, the way she'd said, "She's this rock in my heart, do you understand?"

I thought of Jack's rifle.

Suddenly I felt angry at them, Elise and Barbara, for being so foolish, so obvious. I asked, "So why does she stay on so late in the season, anyway? I mean, what's there for her to do out there now?"

Barbara met my anger with her own. "She likes it there."

She likes late-night fucking with her boss' wife, that's what she likes. Suddenly I felt so confused about my loyalty. I was angry at Barbara for torturing Elise, and possibly much worse, putting her in the path of someone's jealous rage.

I glared at Barbara. Her face collapsed, as if to say neither of us has time for a power struggle right now. She said, "Look, I'm asking for your help."

"What do you want me to do?"

"I was hoping Elise was here."

"What, tied up under the bed or something?"

"I don't mean I still think she's here. I had been hoping."

"What do you want me to do?" I repeated.

"Talk to Jack."

"Are you kidding? No way!"

"He might listen to you."

"Talk to him about what?"

"Make him understand he has to get out a search-and-rescue."

I wanted to ask her if she thought Jack knew anything. But I wasn't supposed to know anything myself. Secrets are like big ropes that tie you up. I couldn't struggle out of this one even if I thought I should.

"Okay," I said feeling as if I was walking right into a trap.

I followed Barbara outside. A light snow had begun to fall again, tender little flakes that landed so softly they felt like kisses from the stars. As we reached the backcountry office, the lights were out and Jack was closing up the wood-burning stove.

"Jack," Barbara said. "Tracy thinks you should do something about Elise too."

"Tracy," he said coolly. "Don't you think Elise is entirely capable?"

The office was dark except for a bit of firelight that escaped from the cutouts in the closed wood-burning stove door. A flare-up caused all our faces to look orange, unearthly.

"If it were anyone else," Barbara cried, unable to disguise the tears in her voice, "you'd have been searching twenty-four hours ago."

"Exactly. If it were anyone else. I completely trust Elise." He lingered on the word trust. "She knows what she's doing. If she takes a chance, she takes a chance. Her choice."

I knew then that he knew. Barbara must have known too. He looked at me and in his face I saw what so many people admired in Jack. It was something deeper than pride, deeper maybe even than love. It was a fierce tenacity. He had what he wanted and somewhere in life he'd learned that what matters most is holding on. Even if it meant going too far sometimes, way too far.

"Jack," I said.

"Don't you agree, Tracy?" Jack said slowly. "Don't you think

Elise can take care of herself?"

"No, Jack," I said. "I don't think so. Not necessarily."

"Then go find her. You two go find her."

Barbara's tears hissed out of her, like steam from a pressure cooker. She ran out the door. I began to follow her but then stopped and looked again at Jack. With the door closed on the stove, the fire had gone out quickly. It was dark in the back country office. I could only see the sheen of his eyes, the line of his mouth. I wanted to ask if he knew where Elise was, but he wouldn't tell me even if he did. Jack knew how to live his passions without leaving a shred of evidence.

I ran out after Barbara. I knew she was going back to Mount Fremont right away, to look for Elise. "Wait one second," I called after her. "I'm coming with you."

I stopped in my cabin and grabbed my parka. When I came back out, Barbara was already on the trail, halfway up Sourdough Ridge. She ran almost the entire way out to Frozen Lake and wouldn't wait for me to catch up with her. At the fork in the trail, she leaned against the wooden post holding up the sign that pointed in three directions—up to Burroughs Mountain, up in the opposite direction to Mount Fremont, and between the two mountains, down to Berkeley Park. She was doubled over, gasping for oxygen. Just as I got there she took off again, her long legs climbing the long trail across the face of Mount Fremont to the top.

I couldn't see the fire tower tonight. The snow fuzzed up the view and no lantern burned from inside the glass room. Finally, at the top, I caught up with Barbara who stood beside one of the tower's legs, sucking in the cold air. The light snow had made a lace mantilla on her head. She spun around in a couple of circles, as if we might discover Elise collapsed in the soil right there under the tower. Then she cupped her hands and shouted, "Elise! Elise!"

The falling snow muted her voice. I watched Barbara gaze down into the valley toward Berkeley Park. "Sometimes," she heaved for air. She pointed down to the grassy meadows below, now covered with a fine layer of snow. "Sometimes . . ."

She couldn't finish the sentence, but somehow I understood, or thought I did, what she was trying to say. Sometimes she and Elise made love down in Berkeley Park. I was glad to hear it, glad to know they didn't always do it in the tower, with the lantern lit, in plain view.

Then, suddenly, Barbara started crashing down the hill toward the snow-covered meadows. I knew I should stop her, calm her down. We had to make a plan, be rational in this search. I didn't want to spend the night chasing Barbara.

"Barbara!" I shouted, but she kept plunging down the hillside, the distance between us growing.

Then I heard the dense, muffled knocking sound. At first I thought it was the wind, or maybe a rock loosening and starting to roll, but the sound was right above me. A knocking inside the tower. For half a second I worried about Barbara, then I chased up the tower stairs. The door was ajar and I shoved through it.

A moaning lump lay in the sleeping bag on the cot. I knelt down beside her and pulled back the top of the bag. Her clothes were soaking wet. Elise grunted, as if my peeling back the sleeping bag hurt. She garbled out some words I couldn't understand. I quickly found the lantern, lit it, and held it over her body. Blood matted her hair and a deep gash on her cheek looked wet and infected. I set the lantern on the map table and gently loosened her clothing. Elise's entire body was bruised. Even through her jeans you could see that one knee was swollen to the size of a cantaloupe.

"Babba . . ."

"It's me, Tracy."

"Babba. I want."

"You want Barbara," I translated, then told her, "No you don't. Elise, I love you." Finding a water bottle on the floor I nudged an arm under her shoulders and dripped some water onto her lips. "Barbara is useless to you," I told her. "I'm the one who loves you." I stroked the bloody hair off her forehead, but I didn't kiss her. "Listen to me, Elise. You're nuts to carry on like this with Barbara. Someone's gonna get hurt, really hurt—"

At this her mouth wrenched into what I guessed was a smile. She grunted a laugh. "Hurt," she said. "Yeah, someun hurt."

Elise and I both heard the footsteps pounding up the stairs. Barbara must have seen the lantern light from below and returned. "Believe me," I told Elise, "you don't know what good loving is. Give me a chance." But her eyes had rolled toward the door. Barbara lunged in.

"Elise!" Barbara shrieked, rushing over. "Oh, sweetheart, oh, my darling." She fell onto her knees by the cot and pushed me aside with her whole body. "Oh god," she whispered, seeing the bruises, the knee, the blood. Barbara stroked her lover's arms, belly, thighs, kissed her bloody cheek. Then she sobbed, demanded an explanation.

Through the thickness of her pain I understood some of Elise's words, "The bears. Goodbye. For the winter. A cliff."

"What bears?" Barbara asked. "What are you talking about?"

A warmth washed over me and I laughed, I laughed hard, in relief and in acknowledging the gift. Elise was badly hurt, but she was alive. And I had just learned that the bears were something she'd given to me and me alone. Barbara didn't know about the bears.

I asked Elise, "Did you go over to where you think their den is?"

Barbara jerked around to glare at me. "What bears?"

Elise nodded.

"And you fell?"

Another nod. "Cliff. Fiffy feet."

"Oh, Elise," I said, kneeling beside Barbara again. "How did you get back here?"

No answer.

"You dragged yourself, didn't you?"

A yes nod.

"*What* bears?" Barbara said again. "Why didn't you call us on the radio?"

"Soon," Elise mumbled. "Tying ta talk."

"I think she just got here," I said. "Her clothes are wet. She probably wanted to warm up first." Which was smart. She was lucky she wasn't dead of hypothermia.

I reached over Barbara and touched Elise's cheek with the back of my hand, like I had the last time I saw her. "And did you see the bears, Elise?"

She moved her head to the side, grunted, "N—"

"Forget the bears," Barbara said. "One of us has to go get help. I'll stay with Elise. You go."

I almost said, *Let's ask Elise which of us she wants to stay and which to go*, but it would have been a dumb question. We all knew the answer. Besides, something hard washed out of me with that laughter. I could walk away from Elise now, I had to anyway, but I also felt that I could. I glanced out the windows of the tower and saw that, although it was still snowing a bit, great gaps of clear sky had opened up, exposing the clean, bare surface of the nearly full moon. Something inside me rocketed past the ache at the back of my throat to that starry wilderness she'd shown me. It was the place before language, the place where stories came from, where life comes from. I said, "Elise, you're about the best thing I've come across my whole life."

She was silent, but I could see her panic, even through the blood and pain. Her whole body convulsed as if she wanted to fend me off. I knew she was afraid I'd reveal our intimacy to Barbara. And how I wanted to!

"Don't worry," I said as I stood up and pulled the sleeping bag back over her shivering body. "I'm leaving. I just wanted to thank you."

I looked at Barbara. I wasn't feeling so free that I didn't want to have the last word with her. "You stay here," I ordered. "I'll go get help."

I ran back to Sunrise as fast I could in my exhaustion. The sky was clearing and I heard several avalanches slide off the face of Rainier as the fresh snow settled. I went straight to the back country office and slowly opened the door. Jack sat in the dark in the rocker. The office had gone stone cold.

"Barbara?" he said softly.

I was tired of everyone wanting me to be Barbara. "No, not Barbara," I said. "It's Tracy."

He didn't speak, so I went on. "Elise is hurt, but she's okay. She took a bad fall. She somehow got herself back to the tower. She was there when we arrived."

"I told you she could take care of herself," he said. Then, in a little sing-song voice, "Well, thank god there's not *four* deaths on the mountain this year."

I sat down in Jack's desk chair. "What if she hadn't appeared, Jack? Would you have let her die?"

I heard a long sigh in the dark. "I hope not," he said quietly. "I sure hope I wouldn't do that." He rocked gently back and forth in the rocker. It was so cold and quiet I could hear him breathing.

"Better get a stretcher up there," I said. "She can't walk."

"Okay."

I waited while he stood and walked over to the desk. He wavered there a moment.

I said, "Do it," and he reached for the radio.

I am back with the interpretive staff at Sunrise this summer. Jack is back and so is Barbara. No one inhabits the fire tower. Just like Jack said, Elise was the last of a dying breed. No one could ever fill her shoes.

Jack is changed. It's subtle, no big deal, but it's as if he's lost some elasticity. Or maybe electricity. Somehow I imagine him feeling that even though he has Barbara and Elise is gone, that somehow he still got the consolation prize. I wish we could go out for double shots of Scotch again this year though I'm confident it won't happen.

At the beginning-of-the-season cookout, I managed to get Barbara alone for a second and dared to ask if she'd heard from Elise. She looked at me coolly, as if I'd asked the rudest question, and didn't answer. I suspect she hasn't heard from her.

I didn't see Elise again after leaving her and Barbara in the tower last September. By the time the rescue team got her back to Sunrise it was four in the morning and I'd fallen asleep. They drove her straight to the hospital in town. I thought about stopping to see her when I drove home to Seattle the next day, but I didn't.

We've only been on the mountain a couple of weeks so far this year. Maybe things will change, but for now Barbara keeps her distance from me, though she is slightly more communicative than she was last summer. Sometimes I want to tell her, "Elise and I only made love once."

But oh that once.

Besides, I do believe, and think that Barbara must also know, that what happened between me and Elise had something to do with Elise finally moving on.

Yesterday, an unseasonably hot June afternoon, I walked out to Mount Fremont. Patches of snow still covered a lot of the trail, but rivers ran off them. They'll be gone by the end of the week.

The glass room at the top of the tower was boarded up. I sat on the stairs and looked out, away from the mountain, at the faraway view. I must have sat very still for a long time because the bears got close enough to startle me.

The sow had a brown spot on the right side of her nose and her front paws were so pigeon-toed it was a wonder she could walk without tripping. Her two cubs, now well over a year old, mature enough to be fairly independent, scuffled along at a good distance from their mama.

All three bears noticed me noticing them. The sow lifted her nose in the air and swung it back and forth, smelling.

"Sorry, old girl," I whispered. "I'm not her."

The bears turned and lumbered back down the embankment toward Berkeley Park. I felt overwhelmed with the sadness I imagined the sow must feel. "I miss her too," I called after the bears.

Then I looked up at the mountain, grandly filling half the sky, so immovable and stately in her uniform of blue-white glaciers. It was all an act, though, because I knew her heart bubbled with liquid heat.

ABOUT THE AUTHOR

Lucy Jane Bledsoe's stories have appeared in *Another Wilderness* (Seal, 1994), *Sister and Brother* (HarperSanFrancisco, 1994), *Sportsdykes* (St. Martin's, 1994), *Growing Up Gay* (The New Press, 1993), *Women on Women 2* (Plume, 1993) and *AfterGlow* (Alyson, 1993). Her writing has appeared in numerous magazines including *Fiction International, Newsday Magazine, Girljock, Northwest Literary Forum, Evergreen Chronicles, Conditions* and *Focus.* She has edited several anthologies including *Goddesses We Ain't: Tenderloin Women Writers* (Freedom Voices, 1992), funded by a San Francisco Women's Foundation grant, *Let the Spirit Flow,* with Pam Nicholls (Berkeley Reads, 1995) and *Hot Licks* (Alyson, 1995). She has received a National Endowment for the Humanities Youthgrant and the PEN Syndicated Fiction Award. She works as a writer and teaches creative writing workshops for adult literacy programs in the Bay Area. *Sweat* is her first collection of short fiction.

OTHER LESBIAN TITLES FROM SEAL PRESS

THE ME IN THE MIRROR by Connie Panzarino. $12.95, 1-878067-45-1. The memoir of writer, lesbian and disability rights activist and artist Connie Panzarino, who has been living with a rare muscular disease since birth.

ALMA ROSE by Edith Forbes. $10.95, 1-878067-33-8. A brilliant lesbian novel filled with unforgettable characters and the vibrant spirit of the West.

OUT OF TIME by Paula Martinac. $9.95, 0-931188-91-1. A delightful and thoughtful novel about lesbian history and the power of memory. *Winner of the 1990 Lambda Literary Award for Best Lesbian Fiction.*

HOME MOVIES by Paula Martinac. $10.95, 1-878067-32-X. This timely story charts the emotional terrain of losing a loved one to AIDS and the intricacies of personal and family relationships.

MARGINS by Terri de la Peña. $10.95, 1-878067-19-2. An insightful story about family relationships, recovery from loss, creativity and lesbian passion.

LOVERS' CHOICE by Becky Birtha. $10.95, 1-878067-41-9. Provocative stories charting the course of women's lives by an important Black lesbian feminist writer.

CEREMONIES OF THE HEART: *Celebrating Lesbian Unions* edited by Becky Butler. $14.95, 0-931188-92-X. An anthology of twenty-five personal accounts of ceremonies of commitment, from the momentous decision to the day of celebration.

LESBIAN COUPLES: *Creating Healthy Relationships for the 90s* by D. Merilee Clunis and G. Dorsey Green. $12.95, 1-878067-37-0. The first definitive guide for lesbians that describes the pleasures and challenges of being part of a couple. Also available on audiocassette, $9.95, 0-931188-85-7.

THE LESBIAN PARENTING BOOK: *A Guide to Creating Families and Raising Children* by D. Merilee Clunis and G. Dorsey Green. $16.95, 1-878067-68-0. This practical and readable book covers a wide range of parenting topics as well as issues specifically relevant to lesbian families. Information on each child development stage is also provided.

SEAL PRESS publishes many books by women writers under the categories of women's studies, fiction, translations, young adult and children, parenting, self-help, recovery and health, and women in sports and the outdoors. To receive a free catalog or to order directly, write to us at 3131 Western Avenue, Suite 410, Seattle, Washington 98121. Please include 16.5% of total book order for shipping and handling. Thanks!